A WAR FOR MUTANTS

THE NEW SOLDIER

ALBERTO CRUZ PÉREZ

Copyright © 2023 by Alberto Cruz Pérez

All rights reserved.

No part of this book may be reproduced in any form or by any form or by any electronic or mechanical means, including information storage and retrieval systems without written permission from the author, except for the use of brief quotations in a book review.

ISBN 979-8-9883328-0-0 (Paperback Edition)
ISBN 979-8-9883328-1-7 (E-book)

Cover art by Rashed AlAkroka
Edited by Joseph Furmanick
Interior by Alberto Cruz Pérez

*To my family and friends,
who inspire me to thrive with the story.*

A WAR FOR MUTANTS

THE NEW SOLDIER

CHAPTER ONE

"Man down!" someone shouted. A soldier's head was blown to pieces.

"Take cover!" a captain screamed to a small group of soldiers. The sound of bullets grew closer, stray rounds hitting the blocks of cement they hid behind. Only the captain and six soldiers were left. They crouched, quickly hiding behind the debris. The local houses and buildings had been destroyed in what remained of the city of Scateror.

"ENEMY SIGHTED… SEVEN ART GUN TROOPS REMAINING…" a robot spoke with the voice of an old radio, as it shot bullets from its hand like a machine gun. It was very wide and covered from head to toe with strange metal that was painted with blue and orange stripes at the edge of each piece. One of the soldiers grabbed a grenade from his waist, pulled the trigger and threw it at the robot. It hit the target and exploded.

The robot stopped shooting, and everyone stood up to see.

There was smoke all over the place, but after a few tense seconds it finally faded. The soldiers were dismayed to see that no damage was done to the robot. The captain and the soldiers raised their rifles and started shooting. Some bullets managed to dent the metal, while others bounced off the robot. Unfortunately for the humans, none made a direct hit. They hid back into cover, looking for ammunition to reload with. The robot began shooting again.

"Now these robots can talk?" a soldier shouted, while returning fire. "Last time I checked these metal heads couldn't speak!"

"Probably an upgrade so they could communicate with Sentry Run's soldiers," the captain mused while reloading his gun.

"It would've been very helpful if we knew about this sooner…" The soldier shouted, "I'm almost out of bullets! I thought there weren't any more of these bastards! At this rate, we'll be killed if we don't eliminate that robot fast!"

"Luckily there's only one," another soldier spoke. He stood from his cover to put another burst into the robot, but shortly into the barrage the rifle stopped and made a clicking sound. He was out of bullets. Quickly taking cover, he searched for another magazine to reload with. None left. No grenades either. Nothing to fight back against the robot. He looked at his surroundings; there wasn't anything left to use as cover. Only the dead bodies of fallen soldiers and the remains of robots, divided into many pieces, decorated the landscape. If they tried to make a run for it, the robot would have a clear view to shoot them on the spot. They were trapped.

One of the soldiers put his rifle down, accepting his defeat.

He took a cigar and a lighter out of his pocket, lit it, and started smoking. "Well, if we die, might as well enjoy my last smoke."

"You got another one, mate?" another soldier asked.

The captain stood up alone and aimed at the robot's head. It had a sensor—a horizontal red line spanning its head—with which the robot could detect anyone in sight. The captain shot his remaining bullets, emptying his magazine. One bullet clipped a corner of the sensor, stunning the robot for a moment. "We won't die here!" he shouted. "We will keep hitting it with everything we got!"

The robot recovered from the stun and put its arms together, forming a bigger weapon. The captain could see the robot aiming at where they were taking cover, charging a strange energy on this new weapon. It looked deadly; like it could kill them with one shot. The captain tried to reach for a backup magazine from the pockets on his uniform, but there were none left. He was also out of bullets.

The captain quickly hid behind the debris, crouching next to his soldiers and breathing heavily. He tried to calm himself to speak with the others. "I take it back…" he said, shame in his voice. He accepted that this would be his death but knew that he was still in charge of these men. He turned his head to look at the soldiers. They were afraid, visibly scared, but none of them were panicked. It seemed that they had also accepted their fate, that this would be the end for them. The captain chuckled once. "Mind passing me a cigar?" he asked a soldier.

The sound coming from the robot's weapon changed as it appeared to finish its charge. "ENERGY BULLET COMPLET-

ED," the robot announced. "READY TO SHOOT IN FIVE... FOUR... THREE... TWO... ONE..." *BAM!* The energy bullet passed the soldiers, crackling through the air to strike another location. An explosion occurred when it hit, making a wave of pressure strong enough to force everyone to cover their eyes from the dust. When the wind passed, the captain and the soldiers stood up to observe the robot.

It lay on the ground. A giant boulder, which had not been there before, was now next to it. The robot's right arm was squished; crushed in several places on the side of the boulder.

"ALERT... MUTANT ON SIGHT..." the robot announced. It shifted, shooting in what seemed to be a random direction—one away from the soldiers. The captain followed the robot's aim, but with the smoke spreading around wasn't able to see anyone. Through the dust, though, there was something—the captain noticed something shining, like a pair of red, glowing eyes.

The robot quickly charged an energy bullet with one arm and shot a giant blast in that direction. Another huge impact made the wind surge through their surroundings. The captain and the soldiers hid behind the debris, covering themselves from the incoming dust.

"What's going on?" one soldier asked, panic creeping into his voice.

"I don't know, I thought there weren't any survivors left in the city," the captain replied. When the wind pressure faded, they peered carefully at the robot again. The captain couldn't find those strange red eyes, and believed the robot must have blown up the mutant. He turned around, facing where the soldiers were hiding, slowly walking back to them.

"ART GUN TROOPS LOCATED… EXTERMINATE… EXTERMINATE!" The robot was getting closer and closer to the soldiers. "EXTERMINATE… EXT—" Something cut the robot off. Another boulder, smaller but still formidable, passed clear through his chest and crashed to the ground in front of the soldiers. The robot fell flatly to the ground, defeated. The captain and his soldiers walked from their hideout, aiming with their rifles while cautiously advancing.

"Is it safe? I mean we don't have any bull—"

"Shh," the captain shushed the soldier. "Keep moving." When they reached the robot, it was completely destroyed on the inside. Oils dripped and a tangle of cables were spread messily on one side of the hole in the chest. It wouldn't stand again anytime soon. Everyone heard a growling noise and quickly aimed their empty weapons where it came from as the strange, red shining eyes appeared again.

Approaching slowly, the shining eyes faded. The body they were attached to became visible as it got closer to the soldiers. It was a survivor, a boy. He took a few hesitant steps closer but fainted and fell to the ground. The captain and the soldiers ran toward the boy, then turned him over.

"He's been injured. Find something to treat his wounds… Now!" a soldier shouted. Another soldier knelt, laying his rifle down looking through his backpack for first-aid supplies. The captain, on the other hand, checked the perimeter to see if any more surprises might come. But it looked like they were clear of danger. He called for an extraction, requesting to be picked up in Scateror while another soldier took a closer look at the boy.

At first glance, he seemed like a normal teenager with dark shoulder length hair. He was thin and wore a black shirt and short pants. His normalcy vanished when the boy opened his eyes slightly; they were dark red, a color probably never before seen on a person. The soldier took stock of the boy's injuries: he was bleeding from his forehead and had cuts and bruises all over his body. At first, he looked calm, but terror immediately washed over him as he started breathing heavily and panicking.

"It's all right. You're in good hands. We're getting you out of here as soon as possible," spoke the soldier who was helping the boy. Everyone had the same questions in their heads: who was he? How was he still alive after the massacre in Scateror? What abilities had he used to survive?

In any case, what mattered now was that he was safe. The captain signaled with his hand, giving the order to bring the survivor with them. The soldier helped the boy stand, gently lifting him with his arms until he could stand up by himself. "Come, we're going to get you somewhere safe," the soldier said, trying to calm his nerves. "Do you have a name?"

"My name..." he took his time answering, trying not to make eye contact. He appeared to be traumatized and it seemed hard for him to speak. After a few quiet moments, he finally answered. "My name... is Zenrot."

"Well, Zenrot, we're going to get you home," the soldier said. The captain approached to share the news.

"I've called in an extraction point to pick us up and get us back to base. We need to inform Arashi that we found a survivor."

They went to a safe spot to hide while they waited, a nearby building with high, broken walls but no roof. A soldier took a small towel, added some water from his bottle, and handed it to Zenrot so he could clean the blood from his head. Zenrot was nervous, but gently took the towel and rubbed it on his forehead. Everyone waited for extraction and, almost half an hour later, they heard something approach. A truck had finally arrived.

"Let's get going. Arashi doesn't like to wait." The captain spoke softly, yet there were nerves in his voice. "You don't want to see him when he's pissed."

They moved to the truck, guarding Zenrot as if they were his bodyguards. A few soldiers boarded the truck from the back, then the others helped Zenrot before boarding behind him. Once everyone was inside, the truck started running and slowly moved away from the city. Zenrot watched from the back of the truck, though he could barely see the sky with the fire and smoke coming out of the buildings; some were actively crumbling as they passed. Vehicles were crushed, streetlights bent, and debris was all over the streets. There were many dead bodies in the field. He saw soldiers with the same uniform as those who recused him, apparently blown into pieces. There were what must have been civilians who had lived in Scateror, shot and left where they fell. People with family, with children—all gone. There was nothing left of the city.

There weren't just bodies. There were also robots in pieces. As the truck shakily moved, Zenrot noticed a symbol on one of the robots' arms. He couldn't see much detail, but he saw a shield with a white stroke outside and, on the inside, a blue background with a man dashing forward holding a rifle painted in white. Under it, there was a name painted in white and orange: Sentry Run. The name sounded very familiar to Zenrot, but there was only one problem: he didn't remember the robots. Nor could he remember who the soldiers were or why they were helping him.

The truck reached a forest, driving away from the main road to avoid detection. Zenrot looked back at the soldiers inside the truck. On closer inspection, he noticed their left arms had a symbol with a red and black polygon shape. Inside the symbol there was a letter *A* and, under the polygon, the words Art Gun were printed. The only thing Zenrot knew so far was that there was a fight between the two groups, and Art Gun looked like the good guys. Minutes passed by, and there wasn't much communication between the soldiers until one of them decided to break the silence.

"So," spoke one of the soldiers, "what are your abilities?"

"Abilities?" Zenrot asked, confused.

"You know… your powers… like the one you use to defeat the robot."

"Sorry, but I have no idea what you are talking about." Zenrot answered shamefully. Most of the soldiers looked up at him, surprised with his answer.

"You mean, you don't remember?" asked the soldier. Zenrot shook his head, confirming he didn't. "You're serious? How can you not?" The soldier anxiously kept speaking, "Your eyes shined bright red. We also heard a strange growl, and you destroyed that robot like nothing. Most mutants can't even defend themselves against a Golem."

No matter how much detail the soldier gave, it still didn't ring a bell for Zenrot.

"Give the kid a break," the captain interrupted. "He was bleeding from his forehead back when we healed his wounds. Maybe he got hit hard enough to forget. For his sake, I hope the boy remembers something in time, though." The truck started slowing down. "We're here," the captain said.

Zenrot looked through the front of the truck to see outside. Soldiers with rifles in their hands stood in the entrance wearing the same Art Gun uniform. The base had giant walls made of cement and portable barriers. It was enormous; to Zenrot it seemed like a twenty-story building. Looking closely at the top of the walls, he saw steel razor wire covering every spot. One soldier from the entrance approached the driver to identify the vehicle.

After their conversation was settled, the truck started moving again, finally inside the base. Zenrot could see the sunset once inside the base and past the walls. He watched many soldiers either marching, standing guard, or training as the truck rolled deeper into the compound. Other people they passed looked like civilians rescued from different nearby cities. He could see many black tents with the Art Gun logo on the sides. It was also visible on the many small buildings holding refugees or storing weapons and gadgets. Some of the structures were up to five stories tall. Far in the distance, Zenrot noticed many vehicles and helicopters. Soldiers departing, he thought, probably to save civilians from yet another city.

The truck slowed down until it finally stopped. The captain and the soldiers climbed out of the vehicle, leaving Zenrot as the last one getting out. When the truck left, his wandering gaze settled on the tallest building of all on the military base. It was a large, round building about fifteen stories high with the Art Gun symbol at the very top—the same symbol the soldiers had on their uniforms.

The captain looked at Zenrot, then to his soldiers. "Come, we must meet in Arashi's office." He started walking. Zenrot glanced back at the soldiers and one of them made a gesture with the butt of his rifle towards the captain, indicating that Zenrot should follow. Walking into the building, Zenrot noticed groups of soldiers guarding every location and roaming in every direction. Others wore white coats, working behind tables and workbenches. This type ran around desperately, discussing plans and strategies over the piles of blueprints and gadgets all over their desks. Zenrot was more confused than ever. He asked himself what all this racket was, and wondered why he was constantly hearing about fighting against another army. Everything was happening so fast, and things were unclear.

"This is too much... what is actually going on around here?" Zenrot asked, frightened.

"You *really* don't remember..." the captain said, quickly gazing at him over his shoulder. "You just fought against an enemy. An enemy who is trying to kill mutants like you."

"What? Impossible... last thing I remember was..." Zenrot gave a pause to remember something, yet nothing came to his mind. If one were to judge him by his expression at that moment, they would have assumed he had literally forgotten everything.

The captain looked forward as he continued onward. Zenrot and the soldiers followed. "I don't know how much you have forgotten about the situation," the captain said lightly, "but there's a fight against another military company named Sentry Run. They are fighting to exterminate the mutant race and kill anyone who tries to stop that goal. If an ordinary human witnesses a mutant and doesn't report it... they'll execute them as well." They reached an elevator and pressed the call button. "We are the ones who prevent *that* from happening."

"Killing mutants? What are mutants?" Zenrot asked curiously. The soldiers could not believe it. The boy didn't even know what mutants were when he was one himself. Whatever caused the damage to his head must have been strong.

"Living beings with special abilities," one soldier spoke calmly. "Paranormal stuff."

"Most of the mutants were humans, others have been born with those abilities. There's also a type of mutant that looks very different. In reality, they're not like us," another soldier answered, disgust creeping into his voice. The captain gazed over his shoulder, looking at the soldier with irritated eyes.

"Different or not, our purpose is to defend every living species by any means necessary." The elevator doors opened, and the captain faced forward. "If Sentry Run had found you back in Scateror, you'd be dead by now. Though that raises the question... I wonder how you are still alive after the massacre that hit the city."

The captain walked into the elevator as Zenrot and the other soldiers followed. Gulping in fear and starting to shiver, Zenrot felt a little nervous. "What are you going to do with me?" he asked.

"That's what we're about to find out," the captain replied. Once everyone was in the elevator, he pushed a button for the fifteenth floor, the top floor of the building. As they rose, Zenrot looked at the soldiers. They stood firmly, but some looked nervous. The fear in their eyes led him to believe that whoever they were meeting was someone either powerful or simply scary enough of their own accord. Zenrot was about to find out in a few moments. When the elevator reached its destination, the doors slid quietly open.

Every soldier marched straight ahead. Zenrot looked around and noted five soldiers to his left and five on the right. They weren't wearing the same uniform as the soldiers he was following; these guys had heavy gray body armor covering them from head to toe. It made it hard to identify them, and each held a heavy machine gun.

As the group advanced, someone was sitting at the desk straight ahead examining some files. The man seemed to be around fifty, bald, and with a white goatee. His appearance was different from other people Zenrot had seen so far. His uniform was a customized body armor, which looked very advanced and easier to manage when compared to the others he'd seen on the rank-and-file soldiers. He had two men guarding his back. They weren't carrying any weapons besides a pistol on their waist and were dressed in a strange black military uniform.

The captain stopped in front of the desk, with Zenrot standing behind him and the other soldiers still in their loose guard formation around him. The captain lowered his rifle and gave a salute to the older man sitting at his desk. "This is team bravo, rank yellow reporting for duty!" The soldiers behind Zenrot lowered their rifles and saluted as well.

"You're late." The old man spoke from behind the files in his hands. "Better have a good excuse, captain."

"We found a survivor. A mutant, to be precise." He looked back at Zenrot, then to the man behind the desk. "He— He saved us back in Scateror. Fought against one of Sentry Run's strongest Golem-class robots and destroyed it. After that, we noticed the boy was injured and took our time taking care of some of his wounds. However, he has no memory of what he did against the enemy... or any of the war, sir."

That caught his attention and finally caused the papers to drop. He laid his elbows on the desk, putting his hands together in front of his chin and staring very seriously at the captain. "You're telling me... that this boy defeated a Golem, instead of my men?"

"Ye—Yes... My apologies, General Arashi. I'm afraid the enemy was stronger. They've upgraded their equipment. If it wasn't for the boy... we wouldn't have survived." The captain shook between his words, sweating from the fear rising in his guts.

Even if the captain was telling the truth, Arashi didn't seem convinced. "And you're telling me that this boy can't remember anything about the war?" Arashi was irritated and spoke condescendingly. "That's impossible." He picked up a folder, waved it at the captain, then tossed it to the table, disgusted. "This war has been going on for almost twenty years. Someone his age couldn't be unaware of the conflict."

"I also find it hard to believe, general. But the boy had a serious injury on his forehead and lost a lot of blood. We believe that injury may have caused significant memory loss." As Zenrot listened to the conversation, he became more amazed and preoccupied. It was hard to believe that the war had been going on for a long time. Forgetting about something that happened in the last few weeks or months because of the damage in his head would sound more believable. But almost twenty years? There was no way you could forget so much because of some blows to the head. Was there? Either way, it was past the point of guessing now.

Zenrot noticed Arashi was staring seriously at the captain. Without showing any emotion, he tilted his head a little to the right, looking straight to Zenrot. It made him nervous, and he immediately started watching his surroundings, instead; started avoiding eye contact with Arashi. But he didn't allow that, standing up from his chair and walking with a measured pace and his hands behind his back to Zenrot. The captain, without saying a word, stepped aside. Arashi and Zenrot met face to face.

Arashi gazed down. "Look at me, boy." His voice was demanding. Zenrot lifted his head, frightened. Arashi was almost a foot and a half taller than his roughly five-foot-tall frame. "So, what is your name?"

"Zenrot…" he said, nervously and through his teeth. He was shivering, and the chattering of his body made it difficult to focus.

"Your full name," an aggressive tone from Arashi prompted.

"I... I don't... I don't know, sir."

Arashi stared at him long enough to study his body language. "What is the last thing you remember?"

He thought as hard as he could; tried to remember anything he could before the incident back in Scateror. There was something he could almost grasp, hovering at the edges of his mind. "I was running..." Zenrot said. His memories felt like traveling through fog. "I remember someone was trying to hide me. I can't remember who, exactly... and I believe I fell asleep..." Then he turned his head to look at the soldiers. "Next thing I know, I was surrounded by these people."

Arashi noticed something strange about Zenrot. He crouched to look even closer and Zenrot stepped back nervously while the taller man examined his eyes; dark and red-colored eyes, dark as blood. "Those eyes... aren't very common for a mutant. But you aren't just a regular mutant... are you?" No words came in reply from Zenrot. He didn't know what to answer because even he didn't know much about himself. Arashi looked like he saw what he needed to, however, and moved back to the desk to sit at his chair. Looking through the files on his desk, he spoke again to the captain. "We have several units undermanned at the moment, correct?"

"Wha—" He quickly faked a cough. "Um, yes. We need more men, but—"

"Then I want *you* to escort this boy to one of our best trainers. Tomorrow. First thing in the morning," Arashi interrupted.

"But for now, take him somewhere to rest. He must've been through a lot already."

"But sir, are you sure about this?" The captain sounded uncertain. "Perhaps we should study his performance before we make certain decisions—"

"My decision is final. Follow my exact instructions. That's an order. Dismissed."

"Yes, sir." He turned around and looked at Zenrot then quickly pointed to one of his soldiers. "You…" he said, "I want you to take the boy and give him everything he needs. Get him ready for tomorrow." He looked back again at Zenrot, "Congratulations, you're one of us now." Zenrot wanted to talk about the decision they had made, but it didn't look like he had much of a choice. He'd been signed up for the war. He questioned to himself how he could forget about something so huge and dangerous—a war doesn't happen overnight. Leaving no time to think things through, the captain signaled for him to go with the soldier that he was told to follow.

"This way," the soldier said. They reached the elevator, and the soldier pushed the button to go to the main floor. Zenrot felt frightened at what they had planned for tomorrow. He was trying not to panic but it became more difficult with every passing minute. He didn't know what abilities he possessed or how he was supposed to use them. The more he thought about it, the more useless he felt. He supposed he probably would be sent with any ordinary group of recruits to train until he was ready, but either way, just by having met Arashi, he was assured that they would make Zenrot into a useful candidate for the army.

Finally, they reached the first floor and the door sliced open. "Follow me," spoke the soldier. Zenrot recognized him as the soldier who took action to help when he was hurt in the city. His voice was familiar.

"You're the one who helped me back in Scateror... right?" Zenrot clarified.

"That's right."

"...Thank you. For helping me."

"No need. In fact, I'm the one who should thank you," the soldier said. No further words were exchanged at that point; it was hard to keep a conversation with all the noise and reckless people. Once they exited the building, the soldier continued, "If it wasn't for you, me and the rest of the crew would have died back in the city against the Golem."

"...It's strange. I can't remember anything about me fighting against a giant robot. You sure it was me?"

"Well... there wasn't anyone else. When the Golem was struck by an attack there was a large plume of smoke. We could see eyes shining bright red through it. Next thing we saw a boulder going through the robot and when we traced it back ... you walked in with your eyes slowly losing their brightness."

Zenrot stopped walking, and the soldier immediately took notice. He stopped a few steps away, leaving Zenrot space to look at the ground. He was watching a puddle, carefully holding the gaze of his own dark red eyes in the reflection of the water. Not shining, as the soldier had described it, but he was certain the man hadn't been lying. Yet he didn't remember any fight. The captain mentioned that Sentry Run would have killed Zenrot if he was found. That brought more questions to mind. *How did I survive during the attack? Was I hiding? Did I fight for my life? Why can't I remember anything?* Someone walked over the puddle, breaking Zenrot's concentration. Glancing up, he took stock of the scene around them. It looked like many soldiers were heading to a place called The Refilled Stomach.

"We might figure what happened later," the soldier said, breaking the awkward silence, "but for now, I assumed you must be hungry." They could both hear Zenrot's stomach growling.

"Yes, I am. Especially after that creepy stare from the old man Arashi."

The soldier chuckled. "Better be careful what you say about him around here," he said softly. "He isn't a friendly person."

Zenrot gazed back at the building they had just departed. "I've noticed."

Soon the soldier signaled Zenrot to walk with him into The Refilled Stomach. When they got inside, it didn't look as Zenrot expected it to be. It wasn't ugly or mistreated, and he was mesmerized that it looked nice enough for them to eat. Soldiers got in line to pick their food like it was a buffet, and the tables were long enough for everyone to sit next to each other. Each was covered with a black and red tablecloth with the logo of the company in the center.

"Looks good enough?" the soldier asked Zenrot, waiting for a reaction.

"No offense, but I thought it would look uglier," he confessed.

The soldier laughed, quickly covering his mouth with his

hand so the fellows around didn't look at them. As they waited in line for the food, the soldier explained things had been organized in different sections when it came to serving the food. Not only soldiers lived on Art Gun's base, but also citizens from different villages. Humans and mutants who'd been rescued had been brought along to the base for safety until the war was over. Many humans were around, but very few mutants. The soldier estimated that no more than ten to twenty of them had been rescued. It had been difficult for Art Gun to rescue more mutants, and they were giving their best attempt to make everyone feel safe and prove that Art Gun would protect everyone at all costs.

Three people left, picking their food and departing the table one by one. Finally, Zenrot and the soldier were served. They went to a table and found an empty space to sit, facing each other. Zenrot desperately started chewing all the food on his plate. He tore into the meal so fast it was as if he hadn't eaten for days. The soldier held his fork in the air, staring with his eyes wide open in obvious shock at how savagely Zenrot was eating. Putting the fork on the table, the soldier took his helmet off, freeing blond, curly hair that was messy from wearing the helmet for a while. He had white skin, blue eyes, and a sharp nose.

"By the way," Zenrot spoke with his mouth full, "I never got the chance to know your name."

"Oh! Well... the name is Brandolf," he said confidently, grabbing the fork from the table and slowly eating the food on his plate.

Despise the comfort Zenrot was starting to feel, something was bothering him. Looking at Brandolf curiously, he asked,

"Can I ask you something?"

"Sure. Ask away."

Zenrot turned his head, looked at the plate with the fork in his hand, and spun it slowly through his fingers. "Why does Arashi want *me* for battle?" He looked up and met Brandolf's eyes. "If there are civilians living in the base… why not summon them for the war if he needed more men? Surely there has to be more mutants and humans around here willing to fight." Brandolf froze with his mouth full, surprised by Zenrot's words. "Don't get me wrong! I'll fight for those who can't even if I don't have much of a choice. It's just… I can't remember how all this happened. And deciding for me to join the army with you guys on short notice… is just, bizarre."

Brandolf couldn't justify his theory because there weren't many mutants in Art Gun. Most of them didn't have useful abilities for combat. However, Zenrot did have a point. During the conversation between Arashi and the captain, Arashi had asked if they needed more men. So why not call for more civilians to join the force?

Finally swallowing his food, Brandolf answered. "Unfortunately, I don't have an answer… I found it very strange, and so did my captain. The right thing is to give you at least a few days to recover, but if Arashi makes the final decision we can't disobey his orders. This is the first time he's sent a mutant to join our forces so abruptly."

"I see…" He pointed at Brandolf with his fork and said, "So I'll probably be on a squad like you?"

Brandolf smirked, one brow twitching while a fake smile

flitted across his face. He didn't know if he should feel flattered or offended the way Zenrot had said that. "Well, it won't be that easy. You'll be sent for training tomorrow morning. Depending on the results, they will announce what kind of soldier you are going to be. Maybe a soldier like *me*..." he said, pitching his voice while staring at Zenrot before chuckling through the food in his mouth, "or be sent to a special group."

Zenrot paid attention to that last part. "What kind of special group?" Brandolf swallowed his food so he could speak properly and answer the question, yet appeared startled before he spoke. He was focusing his sight on another thing, past the younger man. When Zenrot looked back over his shoulder, he noticed Arashi's bodyguards walking inside the cafeteria. Each one grabbed a tray to serve their own food, not speaking to anyone.

When he turned back, Brandolf, had lowered his head and was eating his food. Zenrot could feel Brandolf was tense and trying to avoid contact with them. Maybe it was because he was being too polite, or maybe worried that he could be punished for taking too much time. Maybe Zenrot was overthinking about it... Either way, something felt strange.

Brandolf looked up to Zenrot. "A question for another day..." then stifled a small laugh, finishing his plate and standing up with his tray. "We better get moving. I need to get you ready for tomorrow."

Zenrot finished his tray, stretched his arms, then tapped once on his stomach. He felt relieved for eating such good food. "All right." He stood up with his tray in hand, went to the trash can, shook his tray over it, then stacked it with all the other used trays. "After a good meal, I could definitely use a bath right now."

"I totally agree." Brandolf sniffed a couple of times, hard enough so Zenrot could hear. "'Cause right now, you smell horrible."

"Geez, thanks," he replied sarcastically.

Brandolf gave a soft laugh. "Well, I'm just being honest." He walked with Zenrot towards the door. "But that's nothing. Tomorrow it will get a lot worse."

CHAPTER TWO

The next day, around one o'clock in the morning, Arashi was working in his office on the next plan to attack Sentry Run. Only he and his two bodyguards were in the room. The other soldiers were either on duty outside the building or sleeping for the night. At the sound of the elevator, Arashi glanced up to see who it was. A chubby old man, bald with white and brown hair around the sides of his head, and brown eyes walked out. He was wearing glasses high on his round nose and a lab coat. There was a notebook in his hand and, mumbling, he scribbled notes into it as he approached the desk. Arashi put down the files, half-folded, and steepled his hands on the desk while staring at the old man.

"Mojo Denavor," he said before taking a deep breath and adding, "don't you ever sleep? From what I've heard, you have been working for three days straight without any break to sleep or even eat." Arashi's face wrinkled at the increasingly disturbing odor carried on the other man as Mojo approached. "You could at least take a shower."

Whispering to himself, Mojo finally snapped, "Well my apologies Arashi… it is hard to keep track when I'm just so excited to work on the new subjects for my experiments."

"You should be working on new defenses against Sentry Run technologies," Arashi spat.

"And I am, my general." He slowly walked to the side of Arashi's desk. "But unfortunately, all the materials you have delivered to my lab—the weapons, their robotic parts—aren't going to cut it. Sure, I have found a thing or two, but—"

"But what?"

"We need materials that aren't in terrible condition to examine more thoroughly. It'd be easier if we had actual intel—from the source. That way we can find the robots' weak spot and create a weapon to exploit it. Maybe even one strong enough to destroy any threat."

Arashi looked directly at Mojo without blinking, certain that he was up to something. "I assume you have a suggestion…"

Mojo stopped walking. "I say we attack Sentry Run's headquarters, directly. Before they strike another city."

Arashi jumped to his feet, furious. "Are you out of your damn mind?" Mojo jumped away, fear causing his entire body to visibly shake. "We only won our last fight in Scateror because someone else destroyed the last Golem!"

"Someone?" Mojo asked curiously. "Was it a mutant? Did you find a survivor?" The scientist did a poor job hiding his intrigue.

"That isn't your concern, Mojo."

"Geez, Arashi, no need to be rude." Giggling in a way that

was creepy even to Arashi, Mojo was trying to control his fear. "Back on to the subject, though. Think about it. If we attacked their headquarters directly, Sentry Run wouldn't expect it. They'll believe we're in a different territory saving lives. We just need to find the right moment, so we can send the strongest team to attack while we have another group of soldiers fighting elsewhere." Rubbing his chin with his fingers, he searched for a solution. "Maybe we can send the mutants to attack... what about sending the MSF squad?"

Arashi sat back on his desk, rubbing his forehead with his fingers. He was frustrated with the idea. "Unfortunately, we don't have enough soldiers to send them into the battlefield yet. Besides... the mutants are not ready."

"If it's the number of members you're worried about, I could make another—"

"That's out of the question, Denavor!" Arashi slammed his hands on the desk. "Last time I checked, you made that decision without consulting me and almost screwed everything up with your 'experiments.' I will not take that chance again. Be grateful that you still have your post as director of science and research." Resetting things on his desk, Arashi started organizing his files. Mojo saw the half folder with an MSF stamp on it, and the name written next to that stamp which he had never heard before. *Zenrot*. Mojo grew even more suspicious.

"Ahh... so you did find a mutant in Scateror."

"Mind your business, Mojo."

"Is it the kid I've heard so much about? It's been a while since we found an actual mutant."

"It's none of your concern," Arashi said as he put the files away in a heavy desk drawer, slid it shut, and locked it, "and you better stay away from him." He slowly stood from his chair, and the guards silently moved aside so he could pass. He paced toward the windows of his office. "Besides that, it's not a guarantee that he's qualified for the battlefield."

"Then why did you stamp the MSF initials if you're not even sure he's qualified for one?"

Arashi exhaled in irritation. "You really are a sketchy one. Because, my fellow scientist," the general said while looking through the glass window at the whole base, "I was informed he struck out a Golem by throwing a giant boulder through its chest. Destroyed it with one throw. That isn't something a regular mutant could pull off." He turned around to face Mojo. "At first, I couldn't believe it. Then I looked into his blood red eyes… that's something you don't see on an ordinary mutant, either."

"Then allow me to work on the boy," Mojo said, walking closer to Arashi. "I can figure out what's he's capable of if you just—"

"I already gave you the order to stay away." The general turned away from the scientist, rotating his body a sharp quarter turn back towards the window. "Did I not make myself clear enough?" He glanced back at Mojo directly, the threat clear in his eyes.

"Yes, you did…"

"Good. You're not allowed to go near the boy—or any of the other members of the MSF, for that matter." Arashi raised a hand and snapped his fingers. His bodyguards immediately responded, moving to escort Mojo out. "That will be the end of our conversation for today. I must set a new schedule tomorrow for the boy and I have other priorities in mind."

The bodyguards stepped between Arashi and Mojo, and in return he spun on his heel with an unpleasant expression on his face. The guards followed him until they reached the elevator, but Arashi spoke before they stepped inside.

"Hold up." Startled, Mojo turned to look at him. He was walking away from the window, almost back at his desk. "About the plan you suggested, attacking Sentry Run's headquarters directly... Perhaps we can work something out." A smirk grew across Mojo's face. "Tomorrow we will take time to discuss a strategy and determine the right moment to engage. After the rest of the events I have scheduled, of course. I expect you in the evening, around seven o'clock. Don't keep me waiting." Arashi turned around and walked back to the dark glass of his window.

"As you wish, general." Smiling, Mojo turned and pushed the elevator button. The doors opened and he walked inside, leaving the room without further comment. When the doors closed, Arashi's bodyguards remained guarding the elevator.

Arashi became lost in his thoughts, preoccupied with several competing ideas all at once. He thought about how to solve Sentry Run's invasion in the other cities, of how many people had been lost because of it already, and that, perhaps, Zenrot was the key to form the perfect MSF and end this madness.

"If it goes well," he said to himself, "it could work out for all of us."

***

Twenty minutes before five o'clock in the morning, everyone was sleeping. Zenrot had been taken to one of the spare rooms where the rookies stayed in a converted warehouse full of bunk beds. Zenrot was sleeping in the lower bed, wearing a gray t-shirt, short pants, and white socks. He snored very loudly, disturbing everyone else's sleep.

Five minutes before five o'clock, a group of men stood near Zenrot holding his bedsheet. "All right, ready? One... two... three!" They pulled the sheet hard enough to make Zenrot fall to the floor. The back of his head hit the ground, and he quickly sat up while rubbing the spot that had made contact. He saw his roommates laughing at him. They were all grown men who seemed to be in or around their thirties.

"Morning, sunshine!" one of the soldiers spoke. "Did you sleep well, princess?"

"Princess? He was snoring like a pig," another recruit said mockingly.

"And more, with those... freak show eyes."

The alarm sounded at precisely five o'clock, and everyone left the warehouse in response. *"All recruits must gather on the field in ten minutes,"* said the voice from the intercom. *"I repeat, all recruits on the field in ten minutes."*

"Geez, that is one lousy speaker," Zenrot muttered, pulling on the gray camouflage pants and black boots which had been left for him. There was no time to get well prepared, and he didn't know exactly where he needed to go.

Zenrot ran outside and saw everyone gathering. All the recruits were wearing the same gray uniform; the only difference was that most of the other men looked to be in great shape, and older; everyone looked to be around twenty to thirty years old. Zenrot could feel the tension of the people around him. Some even mumbled to each other while gazing at him. He looked around to see if he could find familiar faces, like Arashi or Brandolf, but none of them were there. There was only him and the other recruits, staring awkwardly.

"Everyone line up!" someone shouted. Every recruit formed a single line, facing forward. An old man approached, wearing a hat and a uniform with a few noticeable badges. He had a large, white mustache on his face and looked to be in his late fifties. Despite his age, he still looked to be in pretty good shape. The old man slowly walked in front of everyone, checking each one of the recruits over. He was small in height compared to the recruits. He stopped in front of Zenrot, looking at him from head to toe, with no expression on his face and no words spoken. After a moment, he kept walking.

Finished examining each recruit, the old man stepped away and stood at a distance from the formation, facing everyone. "Good morning, gentlemen. My name is Major Ryan Venango. Arashi will come down shortly to deliver a message before we begin your training. I see a lot of new faces... even strange ones." Some recruits laughed. Zenrot didn't have to guess it was for him. "Now!" Every recruit snapped to attention. "Some of you might be marksmen. Others can be suppliers, engineers, scientists... whatever Art Gun needs for us to win this war. So, refresh my memory, gentlemen… why are we at war?" One of the men raised his hand and Ryan pointed at him. "Yes, you."

"To protect the innocents in danger! Sir!" the recruit shouted.

"And who are those?" Ryan asked.

"The people—our kind, sir!"

Ryan walked closer until he was face to face with the recruit. "And what do you mean by *our kind*?"

"I—I beg your pardon? Sir?" Mumbling his words, Ryan knew the recruit couldn't give a proper response. He took a few steps back from the recruit and began pacing.

"Our purpose isn't to just defend the weak—which I know to some of you means only the humans. People with no special abilities. But I must remind all of you… we are at war because we're trying our best to save the mutant race," Ryan looked back over the soldiers, gazing at the recruit who answered his question, "not just *our kind*."

The recruit swallowed in fear.

"Saving the mutants?" Zenrot said, thinking out loud. Ryan stopped pacing in front of him, making Zenrot more nervous than ever. He hoped he was not in trouble.

"Correct. This war started because Sentry Run wants to erase all mutants from existence and are willing to kill every person who stands in their way. That include us… the humans."

One of the recruits took a step ahead. "With all due respect, aren't the mutants against humans in the first place?" The recruit spoke firmly as Ryan intently strode toward him, listening. "One mutant massacred a whole city, and another one did the same to a circus show full of people. Their actions are the reason this war even started. Surely you must be aware that not all mutants are worth saving."

Zenrot looked to his left, noticing that the recruit who spoke was one of the guys that pulled him to the ground when he was sleeping. His gaze continued across the other recruits. Judging by their behavior and looks, everyone appeared to be any ordinary human. Zenrot, on the other hand, felt excluded. He was the only mutant standing in the field.

Ryan gestured toward the recruit that spoke, giving them an unpleasant look. "Now I know who will work as a supplier for the rest of the war..." Everyone except Zenrot laughed at the recruit who spoke. "You're right... everything started because a few mutants decided to go against ordinary humans. However, not all mutants think alike. Not all of them are evil. Judging by this man's words, I believe most of you disagree with Art Gun's purpose. I can promise you, gentlemen, this— this is a battle for a greater cause than any other in our history. Our purpose is not only to save those in danger, but also to prevent any madness and cruelty. It may have started with two mutants... maybe more... but now, another military company run only by humans is the one committing all the cruelty: killing innocent mutants who just want a normal life or killing even humans just because some think different. Sentry Run wants to clear the mutant race and take control by giving the world fear. That isn't a way to live a life, gentlemen. We are here to serve so humans and mutants can live together in peace. If another mutant goes out of control, we are the one who will stop them. Not because we're going to show them fear, but because it is the right thing to do. We'll show the world we will stop at nothing to keep peace in our land! That is why you're here to serve, gentlemen. That is what makes us Art Gun: a name and a symbol for justice. Have I made myself clear enough?"

"Yes, sir!" everyone shouted.

"Well, you already said the words of my speech," Arashi said, arriving and standing next to Ryan.

"Ge—General!" Ryan said nervously. "My apologies, General Arashi... I was just—"

Arashi lifted his hand for Ryan to stop speaking and gave a small smile. "No need to explain, Major. Your speech was ten times better than what I had in mind. To be honest, I was practicing in my head while on my way here." Zenrot felt uncertain at how Arashi was behaving with his staff. When he met Arashi back at his office, he had been serious and terrifying deciding what Zenrot's purpose in the base would be. Now, Arashi looked calm and approachable, showing a good image for the recruits.

"Everyone! Meet General Arashi Hatekro. The leader of this base." Everyone stomped their feet twice and saluted by raising their right hand sharply and placing it near their right eye—except for Zenrot. Ryan gazed at him with furious eyes and Zenrot quickly made the same motion. Arashi chuckled at his delayed behavior and then turned to Ryan, whispering in his ear. Once Arashi finished speaking, he fell back, standing firmly. Everyone noticed the look of shocked surprise on Ryan's face.

"Are you sure, sir?" Ryan asked. Arashi nodded, and they

both turned to face the recruits. "Zenrot... Take two steps forward, please." He complied, walking out of the recruits' formation. The major's face became even more shocked. He turned his head towards Arashi again, almost stammering. "Are you sure? Him?"

Arashi nodded, visibly certain of his decision despite Zenrot and the rest of the recruits' confusion at what these two were chattering on about. Ryan looked directly at Zenrot, then turned to the other recruits. "I must inform you all that we are only picking one marksman for battle, and he has been selected. The rest of you will be selected as suppliers, engineers, or scientists. If we need more men in the battlefield, you'll be called upon with short notice."

The recruits weren't pleased about the news. Despite the military precision they had shown with the saluting and coming to attention, everyone devolved into chatting between one another, pissed at what had just happened. "I know it's not part of the protocol to assign you to a role this soon…" Ryan tried to continue, but the recruits were growing more agitated and disgruntled with every second that passed. The situation was getting difficult for the major to handle, and a flash of annoyance flitted across Arashi's face.

"Silence!" He yelled loud enough for everyone to hear over the myriad of side conversations. "This was my decision. I have already chosen who I need for battle."

"An out-of-shape mutant?" one recruit shouted back.

"Sir, with all due respect," another recruit began, "any of us look a lot more in shape and prepared compared to the boy."

Every other recruit present agreed with his words.

"You may be right," Arashi spoke firmly and with a flat tone. He turned his head from side to side, slowly staring at every recruit. "Most of you look well enough to fight as a marksman, I'll give you all that. But unfortunately, I only see ungrateful racists who are against the mutants. Until any of you prove you're worthy, you will stay away from the battlefield and assist as supporters for the base." Then his expression changes to anger. "Does anybody have a problem with that?" he asked more loudly. He was met with pure silence; not a single recruit answered. "Good! Now, Zenrot, you'll begin with Ryan's training shortly. The rest of you will be called later in the afternoon to be shown where you'll work on base. Dismissed."

All the recruits went back to the warehouse with unpleasant looks on their faces. Zenrot was the only one left in the field with Ryan and Arashi. He felt nervous on the inside while standing at attention, posture rigid while he waited for the next command. Ryan started walking around him, exanimating his physical appearance. "We need to get you in shape," the major said, picking up his hair then quickly letting it go. He seemed disgusted by the filthy hair. "And give you a damn haircut!" He stood in front of Zenrot. "Now, we will start with basic training that includes—"

"It won't be basic training for the boy," Arashi interrupted.

Ryan turned his head, looking back at Arashi with confusion. "Then what do you want me to do with him?"

"I want you to train him at MSF level."

"You can't be serious?" He looked back and forth between Zenrot and Arashi, amazed. "He doesn't look anywhere near strong enough for—"

"Are you questioning my decision, Ryan Venango?" the general asked, the threat clear in his voice.

"N –No, sir…" Ryan spoke in return, frightened.

"Good. I need him well trained for the squad. I'll be heading back to my office if you need me." He turned around to face the building and walked away. "Take your time to get Zenrot ready. I'm putting my trust in you, Ryan," he spoke over his shoulder as he left the field.

Zenrot was curious about the name of his training. "MSF? What does that mean?"

Ryan took a deep breath. "It means Mutant Special Force. Well…" He took the top layer of his uniform shirt off. Underneath he was wearing a black, short-sleeved shirt. "Let's get started."

Zenrot raised his eyebrow, face awkward. "For what?"

"Your fighting skills, show me what you can do."

"You want me to hit you?"

"If you can, of course," Ryan said, his tone dripping with casual confidence.

Zenrot gave an awkward smile and said, "I'm not going to fight you."

"What? Afraid to get beaten by an old man?" the major returned, mocking Zenrot to motivate him to fight. "Just because you're a skinny young man, you think that makes you stronger than me? You look like a pile of junk picked up from the garbage with a mop attached to your head."

Zenrot's smile faded, and he found himself moving his

tongue inside his mouth to hide his anger. It was getting difficult for him. His hands slowly turned into fists and his red eyes glowed slightly brighter as he grew angrier. Zenrot snapped and ran towards Ryan to attack. "All right, you asked for it!" He swung a punch with his right hand and missed. Ryan dodged fluidly, moving his body with one leg sliding back. Zenrot almost fell and quickly turned around to attack with a lefthand punch, failing again. He kept throwing punches, multiple at a time, while Ryan continued to dodge his attacks by taking steps back as he moved side to side.

Zenrot approached again and, as he got close enough to strike, Ryan pushed with open hands on Zenrot's wrists to avoid getting hit. Zenrot was getting tired of missing his punches and swung one arm with all his strength to finish Ryan, one way or another. Just when he was about an inch away from finally striking the older man... he missed.

Ryan dodged with a crouch, stepping towards Zenrot and grabbing his wrist. Pulling him closer, Ryan quickly moved aside, putting his leg in front of Zenrot's feet. He pulled back with his leg and, with his other hand on Zenrot's back, pushed him. Zenrot had no choice but to fall. Facing the ground, he turned halfway to his side, swinging his left arm out of anger. Ryan put his weight on top of Zenrot, smoothly grabbing his arm and pushing it to the ground. Then, with his right hand holding Zenrot's neck, the major applied enough tension to Zenrot's body to make him unable to move.

Zenrot was breathing desperately, sweating, and struggling in place. He couldn't even defeat an old man. Ryan, on the other hand, didn't look like he had struggled during the fight. It occurred to Zenrot that this was a small showcase of all the experience he had with combat—this hadn't even been a challenge for him.

"Rule number one: never underestimate your opponent. Especially because of their appearance," Ryan spoke flatly as he delivered the instruction. He let go of Zenrot's arm as he stood up to free him. He offered his hand to help him get up, and Zenrot ground his teeth in annoyance because Ryan was so calm while he was on the ground, embarrassed at his loss. Zenrot accepted his help and stood up.

"We have a lot of work before I even let you get off this base," Ryan spoke as he walked back to grab his uniform top from where he had tossed it to the floor before the fight. Slowly fastening the buttons of his uniform, he looks at Zenrot and walked away. "Follow me," he said moving his hands to behind his back.

Zenrot's red eyes stopped shining as he calmed himself. He began stretching an arm as he followed, walking away from the field and heading onto the streets. His eyes wandered as he followed the older man. There were people sleeping in gray-black tents with the Art Gun logo on top and local stores with food and supplies. Things looked worse as he examined the survivors. Most people didn't look well enough to even stand. Trucks passed at high speed, and Zenrot turned half to the side, wondering what the rush was.

Soldiers hurried from the back of the truck, taking injured people to the emergency room. Others were taking metal junk out and delivering it to Art Gun's main building. Zenrot guessed the metal scrap was from different robots Art Gun had destroyed. Ryan's voice interrupted his observation. "I have a question for you," he said, drawing Zenrot's gaze quickly back to the major. He'd gotten distracted enough that he'd forgotten to walk. "Do you have any family or someone you're close to?"

"I can't say I do," Zenrot answered. "Honestly, I didn't even remember there is a war going on."

Ryan looked over his shoulder. "Really?" He sounded surprised. "Nothing at all?"

"Last thing I remember is when the soldiers treated my wounds back in Scateror…"

"I see. So how do you feel being part of Art Gun?"

"Honestly… scared. Aside from that I'm technically forced to join the army… it's frustrating because I don't have a reason to fight." Ryan stopped, looking over his shoulder and giving a flat stare to Zenrot. "Whoa! Don't get me wrong, I understand Art Gun is fighting for a good cause. It's just… it'd be easier if I remembered something, anything about my past… something that could give me the motivation to stand, you know—I don't know how to explain…" Zenrot tried several ways to express himself in a way for Ryan to understand but no words were coming out of his mouth. The only answer he got was the other man's pale expression, then a slow turn of his head back to the front as Ryan resumed walking. Zenrot followed, embarrassed and feeling like he hadn't properly expressed himself and had insulted what Art Gun believes. The rest of the journey passed in silence as they spent several minutes walking to another part of the base.

"Well, I hope one day you remember something," Ryan finally said as they reached a small building with a glass door in front. He opened the door and entered. "Because in the meantime, you're stuck with me until I say you are ready to fight."

When Zenrot walked inside, he saw a couple of black chairs, mirrors, and sets of drawers attached to the wall. There were electric trimmers on top of the drawers. "What is this?" he asked with a pale face.

"It's a barbershop. The first thing I said that you need is a haircut. You've probably been growing it for a while for it to be at that length, but we need it short. And no, before you ask, you can't just tie it back. I don't care that your hair is straight, it has to be short. We have regulations for a reason, and this is a requirement." Ryan stretched his arm, pointing with an open hand for Zenrot to sit in one of the chairs. "Besides, you look horrible with long hair." Zenrot stared angrily and stomped across the room to sit. One of the workers stepped close and fastened a barber cloth around his neck.

The barber grabbed a pair of scissors and set the hair clippers on his small desk just in case. "So, what type of haircut would you like?" he asked.

"What are my options? Besides being bald and not having many options because of *requirements*," Zenrot said sarcastically. The barber bit his lip, chuckling while holding his laugh in front of Ryan. The barber immediately stopped laughing when he felt threatened by Ryan's expression. He wasn't much of a man for jokes. "Well," Zenrot spoke to interrupt the awkwardness, "can I still have some hair on top at least?" Zenrot thought for a moment what type a haircut he would like, but nothing came to mind. He glanced at the barber, "Can you cut it short and spiky to make me look good? I honestly have no clue; I just don't want to look bald." Then he turned back to Ryan, "I mean... Can I?" The barber looks up to Ryan, waiting for his instructions since he was obviously the one in charge.

"... as long as it follows our protocol."

"Yes! Thanks, Old Man Ryan."

"It's Major Ryan!" he answered, agitated. Then he snapped his fingers, messaging to the barber to start the haircut. "One thing I will teach you during your training is to show some manners." As the barber was cutting Zenrot's hair, Ryan took a notepad out of the inside pocket of his uniform. "All right, this is what we're going to do. We'll start with basic MSF training which consists of the following steps," Ryan opened the notepad and started reading. "500 jumping jacks, 200 push-ups, 500 sit-ups, 100 pull-ups..." As he kept mentioning more and more exercises, Zenrot's eyes were wide open at the immense shock of how much of a workout he was going to have to do.

Even the barber's facial expression said *This boy is screwed.*

"...and they have to be done by the end of the day. If it's not finished, you will run an additional forty-five minutes non-stop around the base." He looked straight at Zenrot. "Any questions?"

"Yeah, is this a joke?" Zenrot asked with a pitched voice.

"Do I look like a comedian?"

"You didn't until now," he said sarcastically. "That's impossible, I can't do all that in a single day. You call that basic training?"

"The more you slack off, the longer it will take for you to finish. Besides, you've been assigned to train as an MSF member. These *are* the basics."

"But I am not even an official member!" Zenrot almost stood up from his chair until the barber grabbed him at the shoulder and sat him back down.

"Easy, mate! Almost left you a bald spot."

"Sorry." Zenrot made eye contact with the barber in the mirror, wincing as he apologized. Holding the hair clippers, the barber continued to cut away at Zenrot's hair as the mutant's eyes turned back to Ryan. "This is insane, I can't do all that. Might as well just tell Arashi I don't want to be any part of this." The barber made a soft laugh, drawing Zenrot's attention back to the man trimming his hair. "What's so funny?"

"I don't think you have the power to make that decision," Ryan answered. "And I wouldn't recommended that you go against his choices."

"And why is that?" Zenrot questioned with a raised eyebrow.

"Because he made the final decision. In case you didn't get the message, there is a war going on. So either you follow my instructions and join us in battle, or Arashi will make sure you regret the decision of turning him down. And trust me," he closed his notepad and returned it to his uniform, "you don't want to be on his bad side."

After minutes of arguing, the barber finally finished cutting Zenrot's hair. He looked at himself in the mirror, checking his head from side to side to see how his haircut looked. It was short on the top with every hair lined up.

"Congratulations, now you look like a man," Ryan said, on his way to the door. "Now it's time to make you one." Zenrot looked pissed and frustrated, thinking of any solution to fight for his reason to leave Art Gun, but Ryan was already outside. Many unfair decisions have been made for Zenrot in a short time. Forced to be a soldier. To train at a mutant level without anyone knowing what he's capable of.

Zenrot was thankful for being helped back at Scatenor but making him fight wasn't something to be grateful for. He heard Ryan shouting, calling for his presence, and looked quickly at the barber and thanked him for his service. Then he walked outside, watching Ryan in the distance standing rigidly. His arms were behind his back with his hands held together.

Zenrot approached and Ryan raised his left arm to look at his watch. "It's 7:30 a.m., we must complete all the exercises I mentioned earlier before 7:00 p.m." Ryan started walking the edge of the avenue and Zenrot followed. "I will decide when you will have a moment to rest."

"What if I fail?"

"You will run forty-five minutes around the base."

"And if I fail *that?*" His curiosity was asking, while he simultaneously hoped there would be some mercy in his answer.

"You will be buried in mud with your head sticking out and stay there for the rest of the night."

Zenrot stopped walking, staring at Ryan with a look of shock at how insane he sounded. "Oh this is bull—"

"Let's start the jumping jacks," Ryan spoke firmly.

"Wait, you mean now?"

"Do I look like I'm screwing around? Yes, now!" Ryan took a whistle out of his uniform pocket and blew it. "Go, go, go!" Zenrot started jumping erratically, moving his hands up and down as if he was a majestic scissor. "That's all you got? I want firm jumping jacks. Straight legs and move your hands up and down. I don't want lame arms! I want those 500 done correctly!"

Zenrot adjusted himself as best he could to please Ryan. Right at about two hundred jumping jacks, his legs started getting tired and he started slowing down. "You aren't stopping here! Faster, faster!" Ryan shouted in Zenrot's ear. The heat of the sun started making it even more difficult. The temperature was hotter than ever, making his uniform all sweaty and his head get dizzy. Biting his tongue between his teeth, he tried to focus. Zenrot lost count of how many jumping jacks he had done. Around twenty minutes later, he stopped, falling to his knees and gasping for breath.

"Did I say you could rest?" Ryan shouted, sounding more pissed than ever. "You missed almost a hundred jumping jacks. That's ten minutes running around base in the dark!" Ryan walked next to Zenrot and pushed him with his leg from the back. "On the ground! It's not even eight o'clock in the morning yet! The day has barely started, give me those 200 push-ups!" He blew his whistle again. Zenrot held himself in position, trying to do his first push-up. His arms started shaking.

"Come on! Back straight and push those arms up and down, don't you dare quit on me! Move, move, move!" Ryan was screaming louder and louder. Zenrot was pushing with all his strength but was sadly going slower and slower. He was tired after doing almost 500 jumping jacks. His sweat dripped on the ground and, as he neared fifty push-ups, he fell completely. Laying on the ground, he watched one or two cars pass by. Soldiers with guns in their hands whispered as they walked past. Zenrot couldn't hear their conversation, but he could tell the soldiers were criticizing him by the look on their faces. Displeased. Disappointment. The worse things he could think of.

Taking his time to rest, Zenrot could hear Ryan's voice in the background yelling and insisting he keep going. He was starting to wonder if he punched Ryan in the face if it would blow his head up because of his strength. After all, he threw a giant boulder through an enemy robot… though he still didn't remember doing that. He hadn't had the opportunity to measure his true strength. Aside from imagining a good relief for himself, he couldn't go against Arashi's plan. Ryan had warned him not to go against the general's will, and he especially wouldn't consider it either since he's a mutant. This war was because some people wanted to eliminate the mutants from existence and going against a military company who wanted a better world between humans and mutants wasn't the smartest plan. Zenrot didn't believe he had any other choice; he must stay for the war.

After taking his moment to think, he started hearing Ryan's words clearly. "…who the hell told you to stop? I don't expect to have a soft mutant! Move it!" Zenrot returned to the starting position, then slowly began giving push-up after push-up. "Come on, keep your head straight!"

Zenrot stopped with his hands on the ground and his body in

the air. His arms were shaking in pain. He fell completely to the ground. "It hurts…"

"You serious? That's all you got? This is what they're making me train? A brat like you?" Ryan crouched a bit and started poking the back of Zenrot's neck. "Come on, you are far from finishing those push-ups. Go, go, go!" Ryan kept screaming, over and over, making Zenrot push his limits. He managed about ten more push-ups, but he fell again to the ground. "For what I see, you'll be running more than 45 minutes in the dark tonight."

"This… is torture," Zenrot spoke, breathing heavily.

"This is just the beginning… and failing is not an option. Now turn around and let's go with 500 sit-ups." Ryan poked Zenrot's back a couple times and stood up. Slowly, Zenrot turned over and bent his knees while his body remained still on the ground. Ryan stood on Zenrot's feet in support. "Come on, hands behind your head. Move it!" Zenrot, holding his hands together at the back of his head, slowly bent his upper body back and forth. This exercise felt a bit easier since it didn't focus as much on his arms. After a hundred and fifty or so sit-ups, however, Zenrot was feeling strange in his stomach. The more sit-up he did, the slower and more painful it was starting to get. Ryan noticed he was slacking and began shouting a fresh round of insults over and over to keep the pressure on him. A half an hour into the regimen, Zenrot was exhausted. He rolled out of the sit-up position, sitting to take a rest.

"Can't we just train back in the field and not on the side of the street?" Zenrot asked.

"First off, when you want to ask me something, you have to

address me by saying, *'Permission to speak, sir?'* Learn some formality." Zenrot chuckled once, finding it a bit hilarious given his present state. "Secondly, you will train wherever I decide to go." Ryan glanced at their surroundings, noticing the soldiers patrolling. "If you're feeling humiliated because people are watching you with disgust in their eyes, then perhaps they should all take a closer look at the unpleasant mutant I'm working with."

Zenrot gasped between his teeth, holding himself from make a wrong choice. He found it ironic that a major who believed in an equal life between humans and mutants kept mistreating and insulting a mutant right in front of him. It could be part of the training, but it didn't convince Zenrot he was doing it because of the training requirements. Yet Zenrot knew he must prove he had worth in a fight, one way or another. If he didn't last long enough to die during the war, he would suffer to death during his training.

CHAPTER THREE

Days passed with Zenrot working a different series of exercises every morning, wearing the same uniform and doing his best on the workout. Unfortunately, he struggled to finish the amount Ryan requested for each exercise. Zenrot was routinely punished by only having fifteen minutes to eat and rest before being sent to train from the very start once again. Every day, until seven o'clock in the evening, Zenrot trained with the other new recruits to complete the amount of exercise required. Some were sent to the battlefield if they were qualified to fight, while others stayed inside the base—required to train further in case Art Gun ran short on soldiers in the field.

Zenrot wasn't even close to be qualified as an MSF, so he had to train with new recruits every day for two hours or until he finished his part of the exercises. Finishing his training by nine o'clock in the evening with the new recruits, Zenrot then had to run forty-five minutes around base for not completing all of his workout in the morning. It felt very unfair, but it would keep happening untul Zenrot succeeded in meeting Ryan's goal. Most people were done working for the night, and only Zenrot was running around the base.

The night was very dark, despite the spotlights aiming into the sky or light poles shining down throughout the base. Zenrot was running in the mud and getting wet because of the rain. Ryan was riding a cart with only two seats, sitting on the passenger side while another soldier was driving slowly to keep up with Zenrot.

"You can jog if you want, but you can't stop moving! So, keep up the pace." Sometimes Zenrot ran for a bit, then jogged to catch his breath. Besides his boot sounding squishy as he ran and the wet sag in the lower part of his pants, it was a perfect opportunity for Zenrot to look deeper into Art Gun. Buildings with multiple floors. Stores that sold food, clothes, accessories, and other articles. Tents where survivors slept. Soldiers performing their usual routine.

As Zenrot jogged forward, looking straight ahead, he said, "Permission to ask a question, sir?" He was deliberately being as polite as he could.

Ryan was impressed he spoke with respect to someone who outranked him. "Permission granted."

"How come there are stores selling things if we're at war?" He had to try hard to maintain his breathing as he jogged while talking to Ryan. "I understand the soldiers may have their privileges, but what about the civilians? There isn't money involved so they can't buy their necessities. How can they earn their stuff?"

"There are civilians giving community services to help Art Gun get stronger. It could be finding supplies outside the base, making new clothes… whatever this place needs to keep it running. If they do that, they're rewarded with recognition for helping Art Gun's community as a credit to each business. They get the best equipment depending on the services they provide."

"I'm surprised they haven't been taken to war." The route he was jogging took a turn and he saw a sector full of helicopters, and artillery machines with soldiers and engineers working on them.

Ryan looked around the base as his vehicle followed. "They have… and many of them died in battle. Most of the people you'll see around are women and children. Some of them have special abilities, but they aren't useful in battle against Sentry Run. If they spot one single mutant, even if it is one categorized with a simple ability, they stop at nothing to wipe it from existence. That's why we're training you. So you can show your true skills in battle and help us defeat these inferiors."

"Pardon my ignorance, sir, but I'm sure you're not training anyone else the same way you're training me."

"You can thank Arashi for that." He looked at his watch, raising his arm to read it well in the dim light. "Well, time's up. That's enough training for today." Ryan dropped his arm as Zenrot stopped jogging and crouched down to rest. The cart stopped next to him. "Before you go, I made a reservation at Art's Grill for you to eat. Feel free to order anything you like. Then head back to the warehouse so you can get some rest for tomorrow's training."

"Is that an order?" Zenrot asked, breathing heavily and turning his head to look at Ryan.

"Going back to the warehouse is mandatory. Although the food is optional, you'll need it if you want to be healthy." He signaled the driver to start the engine. "Don't get any funny ideas to explore. You're not allowed to roam around the base. I expect you tomorrow at the same hour on the field. Don't be late. Dismissed." The cart turned on and traveled on its way.

"Wa—wait!" he yelled, calling out to Ryan, but the major was already long gone. Zenrot was left behind, at night, in the rain. "Great, where the hell is Art's Grill, anyway?" Ryan told him not to explore around the base. Zenrot looked around and couldn't locate the place to eat from where his jog had stopped. He spotted two soldiers patrolling and jogged his way to them before they passed.

"Excuse me, gentlemen!" he called out to the soldiers. When they turned around to see who was getting their attention, one of them started to raise his rifle—Zenrot stopped where he stood as the other soldier grabbed it from the rear sight and lowered the weapon back down. "Didn't mean to scare you," Zenrot spoke lightly, "but I was wondering if you can point me in the right direction to where Art's Grill is located?" Even if Zenrot was asking in the most generous way, he could feel the tension with the soldiers. People in Art Gun may work to save the mutants, but it was clear some people were afraid of them. The way they stared and look to each other made him feel like he was the actual villain.

Fortunately, the soldier that stopped his partner from aiming the rifle told Zenrot to follow, offering to guide him himself until they reached Art's Grill. The other soldier didn't look like he was pleased with the idea, but the first soldier glared at him, then both turned around and started walking. Minutes of travelling through the base later, they finally reached their destination. The soldiers pointed out the local restaurant and headed on their way. Zenrot wanted to thank them for the help, but they looked to be in a hurry. Either they had to continue their patrol duty, or they were trying to get away from Zenrot as soon as possible.

He looked back at the local store. A sign hung on it with the letter *A* of Art Gun's logo and a grill coming out from the center of the letter. The walls and entrance door were made of glass, and he could see the red chairs and black tables from a distance. "Well, it won't be hard to find now," Zenrot said to himself. He walked towards the restaurant and opened the door. A small bell rang on top of the door as he walked in. There was a bar a few feet to his right with a blackboard menu attached to the wall. Tall stools stood next to the bar counter and, in the center of the restaurant, there were a couple of small tables with two chairs each.

"Hey, you!" someone shouted from a distance, drawing Zenrot's attention to where the voice came from. "You're getting water all over my floor!" It was an elderly white man standing behind the bar, almost five feet tall and nearly bald, with white hair just on the sides of his head. His eyes were a bit closed, and he was wearing a chef's coat.

"I'm sorry!" he replied as he raised his open hands to his chest as cover. "Major Ryan sent me here to eat, I just finished training right now."

"Aaahh…" the old man said as he turned to clean the top drawer behind the bar counter. "You're the mutant Ryan told me about." He turned half a side, stretching his arm with his hand pointing at a chair. "Have a seat." Zenrot walked to the counter and sat on one of the stools, his wet clothes still dripping all over the floor. "I'm going to charge Ryan extra for this!" the man said gazing at Zenrot, then the floor, before bending himself to grab something behind the counter. It was a towel. He threw it at Zenrot, hitting him in the face. "Dry yourself up!" the owner said as he turned back to his usual spot. "So, what would you like to drink?"

"Water would be nice."

The owner walked to a small cooler, grabbed a glass next to all the dishes, and poured the water. He walked back to Zenrot and handed it over to him, where Zenrot quickly drank it all in one sip, leaving nothing in the cup. He stretched out his arm with the cup in hand. "Can I have another?" Then, as the elderly man took the cup out of his hand, he added, "You can give me a whole gallon, if you like."

The owner chuckled as he went to a shelf and grabbed a bigger cup, then served him again, "What's your name?" he asked, giving Zenrot the cup filled with water.

"Zenrot, sir." He drank it all in one go again.

"Easy there boy, need to save some for the rest of us," he said in a flat tone.

"Sorry, these workouts were killing me. I've been exercising all day." He looked up to the old man. "Where are my manners…? I haven't asked your name."

He laughed softly. "I can see Ryan has been very strict with you. No need to be sorry for that, name's Marcelo Han. You can call me Mr. Han." He took Zenrot's empty cup and served him water once again. "Right now, there isn't much choice to pick from for food. There's either chicken breast with mashed potatoes or ravioli."

His stomach started rumbling at the mention of good food. "I'll go with the chicken and potatoes."

Mr. Han nodded and walked to the kitchen door in the corner. Both doors opened slightly at a light push, and then Zenrot could hear Mr. Han's voice ordering the food. Minutes later he came back and noticed Zenrot's cup was half full of water. "Saving for the food, huh?" He nodded with his eyes aimed at the cup. "Thought you were thirsty because of the workout."

"I am, but you sounded pretty serious when you said you needed to save water for the other members," he said, embarrassed.

Mr. Han laughed gently. "I was just messing with you. You can drink as much you like. Just make sure you have space for the food. It'll be a shame to see it go to waste for filling yourself up with only water."

"Trust me, I'm starving right now!" He tapped his belly. "I won't let that go to waste." Right in the middle of their conversation, someone came out of the kitchen doors with a plate in hand. A cook placed the plate in front of Zenrot.

"Careful, it's hot," warned the server before they went straight back into the kitchen. Mr. Han handed Zenrot the silverware. Without having the time to blink, Zenrot devoured the food. He didn't even use the knife—just grabbed it with his bare hands and only used his fork for the mashed potatoes. A few seconds later, he had finished his food, practically cleaning his plate. He could even see his reflection on it. Then, without hesitation, Zenrot drank the half cup of water he had saved for last. Mr. Han was impressed that he finished so fast.

"You were *really* hungry after all." He picked up the plate and cup. "Do you need anything else?"

"Nah, I'm good." He burped and rubbed his belly. "Man, that was great! Is this part of being a recruit? Because I can get used to this."

Mr. Han put the plate and cup in the dishwasher, then came back with a small towel and cleaned the counter. "Don't get used to it. Here on Art Gun people don't have much of the privilege you are experiencing right now."

Zenrot looked confused as he raised an eyebrow. "I mean, I've been training nonstop every day. I can even say I've done more than other recruits. It was about time I get some reward for the hard work."

"This isn't a field trip. Remember everyone is fighting right now to survive, and you should be grateful. People aren't exactly the friendly type. I'm surprised Ryan came here and offered you food from *his* merits. Most soldiers and others who are higher ranked only care about themselves. I mean, I can't blame them. It's hard to trust someone else when you're in a war." Zenrot lowered his head.

"Are you sure Ryan is being nice?" he asked, looking to the

side. "Because he sure gave me a hard time—ow!" His forehead was abruptly smacked by Mr. Han's hand. "Why'd you hit me?" he asked as he rubbed his hand on his forehead.

"Because, young lad, he is one of the most respected and loyal officers here in Art Gun! He's fought for many years, leading many armies to survive…" Zenrot got bored as Mr. Han kept talking, laying his arm on the counter and resting his head in his palm. "Are you even listening to me?" Mr. Han shouted angrily.

"Yes." He rolled his eyes as he answered sarcastically. Mr. Han raised his hand again, but Zenrot quickly covered himself under the counter.

"Besides, you should feel proud. Ryan has never allowed anyone else to eat under his account here but you."

Zenrot stood up. "Why me though?" he said, sitting back on the stool. "To be honest, I don't feel like I'm the right candidate. Sure, they've told me I defeated a Golem, but I say it was luck. I don't even know what my abilities are. Only thing I know is that my eyes can shine." Zenrot started raising his voice louder as he spoke, incensed. "And Major Ryan is making me work these ridiculous exercises. This journey has been one pain in the ass!"

"Language!" Mr. Han corrected, raising his hand while holding a towel—ready to smack Zenrot. He flinched but reacted quickly to avoid getting hit.

"Sorry!" Zenrot yelled back. Mr. Han lowered his hand and started wiping the counter with the towel.

"Like I said, you should be grateful. Ryan hasn't been kind to anyone since—" Mr. Han paused, making Zenrot question what he was about to say.

"Since what?" he asked.

"No—nothing. Forget what I said." Mr. Han exhaled. "Listen, you look like a good kid. Believe it or not, Ryan is the best major you can get as a trainer. You should be thankful that it is him and not anyone else. Any other person qualified to train a mutant like you would just do a quick exercise to get over you and hand you over to Arashi. Many people here in base are racist against mutants."

"I noticed that the first day of training…" Zenrot said lightly as he remembered the day the other recruits had bullied him in his sleep. "But does Arashi really need me in battle?"

"Well, like you mentioned before, you did defeat a Golem. That is something that would get his attention. From what I've heard, he's trying to make the strongest mutant squad to defeat Sentry Run. To him, you fit for the team. It's only a matter of time until you're ready. But from what I see, you are far from that."

"Geez, thanks."

"I didn't mean it like you're useless. I'm referring to the fact that you have a lot to learn before you go to the battlefield. Outside the walls of Art Gun is very dangerous. Many soldiers have gone out to fight and very few have returned. Sentry Run are dangerous enemies. You have the chance to train and be the best of mutants before you go out and fight. Some people are sent directly to the battlefield without even proper training. In my opinion, I say Ryan is showing some empathy for you."

Zenrot gave a soft laugh. "I highly doubt it. Ryan has been nothing but strict and bossy to me."

"Well, some people have strange ways to show care and compassion." Mr. Han left the counter and started organizing everything for closing time. "Now, I suggest you go to your warehouse and get some rest. One thing I can assure you, if you think Ryan's exercise today was difficult, it's only going to get worse."

"I can't wait," Zenrot said cynically as he stood up to head to the exit door. "Oh!" He stopped, turning his body half to the side. "Thank you for the meal."

"My pleasure. Hope to see you again. Do stay safe."

Zenrot nodded in gratitude and walked out the door, heading back to the warehouse. There was something that was eating Zenrot's thoughts. Mr. Han mentioned that Ryan has been kind to him. It was hard to believe, but Mr. Han had almost spilled out the truth. Something had happened to the major during his time on the battlefield; something changed him. Zenrot wanted to question Mr. Han on what exactly happened to Ryan to make him the way he was, but it felt out of place to ask. Not to mention that he didn't want to be smacked again. Zenrot would have to be satisfied with the little information he knew.

On arriving at the warehouse, he got himself ready to finally sleep after a long day. Yet he was also preparing himself not to get too comfy mentally—these trainings were going to be happening for quite a long time.

CHAPTER FOUR

"Let's go! On your feet, boy!" Ryan shouted in the field.

Zenrot kept on pushing himself to complete his training. It was the same routine every day at five in the morning. Zenrot had just finished doing diamond push-ups and was now on his way to a pull-up device. Zenrot was supposed to do some pull-ups first, but when he did his first pull-up, the tube bent because of his strength. Art Gun had to make a custom set up with a better tube and stronger metal on the sides to hold the bar just for Zenrot to pull without breaking the equipment. After the pull-ups, Zenrot was assigned to do parallel bar dips. Ryan was on the side, counting every single pull and making sure he finished the entire number of repetitions.

"All right, that's enough! On the ground!" Ryan shouted as Zenrot quickly laid down. "Plank for one minute. Go!"

Zenrot kept his legs as stretched as possible, with his back straight and using his arms as support. Even if the plank was only for a minute, Zenrot started feeling pain in his stomach and slowly lost balance in a matter of seconds. He held his form, though, and even with all the struggling, Zenrot managed to finish the plank.

"All right, let's keep going!" Ryan shouted as he walked away to assign the next exercise.

"Can we get something to eat?" Zenrot asked. "I'm starving."

"You will... once you finish all your exercise for the day." Ryan made sure there was no break. It could take an hour—maybe more—but he wanted Zenrot to focus more on his training. That way, Zenrot wouldn't get distracted or clumsy.

At first, Zenrot found it completely unfair, and felt like he was being mistreated. As the days went by, though, that changed. In the morning, when Zenrot did his workouts and had time to take a break, he noticed the new recruits and watched them training with other mentors. When they were ready, they'd be sent to battle. It was during this time that Zenrot noticed there were also female recruits training with their respective leaders. Some were sent to medical rooms to treat wounded patients; others were sent to battle. Sometimes there wasn't even time, and recruits were sent directly to the battlefield. Art Gun was getting fewer people to fight.

During the night, when Zenrot jogged for failing at his exercises, trucks drove inside the base at full speed and parked next to the medical tents. Soldiers opened the back of the trucks revealing people severely injured, filling the truck with blood. Doctors rushed out with folding cots, laying the wounded soldiers on top of them and quickly bringing them inside for treatment. Things were getting worse.

One night, Ryan drove his cart alone as he watched Zenrot's jogging. He decided to make a stop and give Zenrot a break. He gave him a bottle of water and a sandwich with ham and cheese, covered in foil. Zenrot could've sat on the passenger's seat in the cart, but instead, he sat on the ground. He opened the water bottle and drank it all at once, seemingly oblivious to Ryan's surprise that Zenrot decided to sit on the ground in front of him. Both heard another truck from afar, driving full speed before making a solid stop. It was bringing more wounded soldiers, then sending a fresh batch of fighters inside the same truck back away from the base.

"Permission to speak, sir?" Zenrot spoke as he ripped the foil and ate the sandwich.

"Permission granted."

"Is it really that bad outside these walls?" Zenrot asked through a full mouth, slightly difficult to understand.

"You're going to need to be more specific…"

Zenrot swallowed the food to speak more clearly. "Are we losing the war?"

Ryan gave a small cough. "We're doing our best to stand against Sentry Run's reinforcements. The enemy is getting stronger with the newest army of robots it's built to stand against us."

Zenrot wasn't convinced by his answer. "With all due respect, major," he said in a low voice, "that doesn't answer the real question."

Ryan gave a pause, looking directly at the medical tents where all the soldiers were being tended to. "We are being held back," he finally answered, "but we haven't lost yet. We still have chance to reverse things."

"...and how exactly is Art Gun going to push them back?" Zenrot asked, doubtful.

Ryan turned his face down to Zenrot. "With you, of course. Along with other mutants."

Zenrot coughed, almost choking on the remaining bits of his sandwich. "Sure, tell that to the mutant who hasn't finished all of his training." The sarcasm was heavy in his voice. Zenrot glared at Ryan, but noticed he gave a small laugh. It was the first time Zenrot had ever seen him laughing. He didn't know if the major was pretending for his sake, but it felt wholesome. "I'm surprised Arashi hasn't called for me to join the battlefield."

Ryan's smile fell from his face, his expression returning to its familiar chill. "Oh, he has," Ryan said, catching Zenrot's attention. "It's been a week since your first day of training, and Arashi has been insisting to deliver you so he can put you with the MSF—no matter the current state of your combat skills. But I insisted not to send you away just yet."

"And why is that?"

Ryan looked away to the medical tents. "Because I know you won't survive." He looked in another direction and saw one of the trucks dispatching metal pieces from the robots Art Gun had defeated. "You see those robots, right?" Zenrot nodded. "Those are called the Golems. Looking at some of the other pieces, there is also another type of robot called the Spartans. These robots have been designed to be strong enough to withstand many bullets. Probably even explosions. Their combat skill is also impressive, far beyond what we're prepared for. Not to mention they can charge with incredible force and attack our men without hesitation. To be honest, it is quite frightening."

"And you want to make sure I defeat them all?"

"I want you to live," Ryan answered firmly. "You and every other mutant deserve to have a life of your own. You may have a gift that no other mutant has; to stand for yourself. With enough training, and if we figure out your true abilities, you may stand against anyone in your way. Maybe even inspire others to follow your path. After all, you have progressed quite a lot."

Zenrot turned to look back, shocked at Ryan's words. "*Humph.* Are you really making a compliment towards me? I thought you were a strict major," he joked standing from the ground.

"Don't get funny with me, Zenrot. You still have a lot of work to do before you are ready to fight." He looked at his watch and saw quite a lot of time had passed. "Well, it's time for us to go. I think you'll need more than a cold sandwich after today's work. I made you another reservation at Art's Grill. Looks like you made a good impression on Mr. Han." Zenrot felt a rush of excitement inside because he would taste good food again, though he hoped Mr. Han wouldn't smack him this time. He resolved to be careful with his words. "I must get going, see you tomorrow," Ryan said in dismissal, turning on the cart engine, ready to leave.

"Wa—wait! Major!"

Ryan stomped on the brake, making the cart stop roughly. He turned half around, looking over his shoulder at the younger man. "What is it, Zenrot?" He sounded panicked.

"I wanted to ask if you— if you care— if you are good— if you're—" Zenrot was speaking nervously, struggling to find the right words.

"First, calm down. Second, what are you trying to say?"

Zenrot took a deep breath and finally felt able to speak. He paused, feeling regret at what he was about to say. "Never mind, I forgot what I was going to say." He saluted the major. "My apologies for wasting your time."

Ryan found him confusing, but then he smirked. "No need to be *that* formal." Ryan turned back around. "Go eat at Art's Grill. You need your strength back. Then go to sleep. That's an order." He drove away in the cart, and Zenrot started walking the now-familiar path to the restaurant.

He felt mortified because of the way he spoke to the major. He wanted to ask if Ryan was being kind because he's obligated to, or because he *actually* cared. Zenrot didn't know how to ask about it, though, because it felt it like a personal question—and he was afraid of how his trainer might react. It had been on his mind for a couple of days, ever since Mr. Han had mentioned Ryan only gave from his charity because he cared for Zenrot's wellbeing. Though he couldn't discern exactly why, Zenrot had started to believe what Han said. Even small things seemed to suggest it, like Ryan putting on a smile at a sarcastic comment when he'd never smiled once since their first day working together. Just a few moments ago, Ryan had said it was mandatory to eat at Art's Grill when last time he was told the food was optional. They were small details, but they showed enough. The only problem was what Zenrot really wanted to ask: what had made Ryan change? Why was the major concerned about Zenrot, specifically?

He heard a bell when the door opened. "You're finally here!" Mr. Han shouted, snapping Zenrot out of his thoughts. "Hurry up! Come inside. The food will get cold, and I need to close the shop."

"So-sorry. Ryan and I got busy with running my miles again."

"*Sheesh*. Next time he makes you come at this hour I will smack Ryan myself for making you train so late! I don't care if he's a major! The boy must show some respect."

"Respect to me, or your working hours?"

"BOTH!" he shouted in anger. Zenrot couldn't help it and laughed. Slowly, Mr. Han laughed as well. "Come, this time I made rice with beans on the side—and steak. Ryan left instructions that you eat a good meal this time." With that said, it made one thing clear. Ryan had a strange way to show care for others, but he did care about Zenrot. A singular goal resonated within Zenrot, and that was to win this war. For Ryan, for the mutants, and for anyone else who stood for righteousness.

***

Ninety days had passed. Zenrot had been training five days a week, with two days of rest at the end of the week—though he decided to train on his own on some of those days, anyway. Ryan and many others were quite impressed with Zenrot. He had improved significantly since his first days in Art Gun. He had finally succeeded the immense amount of exercise Ryan had demanded of him. Not only had he done all the push-ups, sit-ups, and other exercises, Zenrot also looked to be in better physical shape. He had grown from a skinny person that looked confused and broken to a very healthy young man with a cut, muscular body. His arms were vascular, his chest and back became ripped, and his legs looked firm for all the miles he had ran at night.

Ryan decided to test Zenrot through extreme events with higher ranked soldiers. The first was flipping truck tires to a certain destination. During that exercise, it was clear that Zenrot had the mutant ability of incredible strength. He flipped the tires like a piece of paper while the other soldiers—who looked both bigger and stronger—struggled at flipping the tire on their second attempt.

Next, Ryan decided to make Zenrot pull a rope against twenty soldiers. Wearing the Art Gun uniform, they all looked twice as strong as Zenrot. He held the rope on one side and the group of soldiers all grabbed on at the other. Whoever lost would need to do community service for the civilians in Art Gun for the rest of the day.

"On your mark…" Everyone held the rope tight. "Ready… Go!" Ryan blew his whistle. The soldiers started pulling the rope with all their strength. The struggle and effort they put in was evident in the gritting of their teeth, the sweat all over their shirts, and the veins showing in their hands and foreheads. Zenrot, on the other end of the rope, stood firm holding the rope with two hands while watching the soldiers doing their best. After a moment he let go of the rope with his left hand, holding on with only his right. He was not even striving against the soldiers.

He turned around while putting the rope up and over his shoulder and, with little apparent effort, walked away as he pulled the rope. The soldiers did their best to resist but couldn't stand against Zenrot's strength. He gave a strong pull, making all soldiers fall on the ground as one.

"Well, you know the drill, boys. Move along!" Ryan shouted, standing with his arms crossed and watching the soldiers walk away with their displeasure at the fact that they needed to work overtime clear on their faces. He turns his head to look at Zenrot, speaking calmly. "You've done well. You earned the remaining hours until afternoon to rest."

"Actually, major," Zenrot spoke as he recovered and coiled the rope to hand over to Ryan, "I was wondering if there's anything I could help with during the day?" Ryan was becoming more impressed with Zenrot of late. Apart from improving his physical shape, he had also improved mentally. His behavior had changed drastically from the confused and whining guy he had started as to a person with a more mature mindset.

"Of course," Ryan answered. "We'll be delivering supplies to the new survivors on my cart." He walked on his way and Zenrot followed.

"That's great! I want to help any people I can before I'm tested this afternoon here on the training field. Today will be the moment of truth to show my skills to help on the battlefield." Zenrot was a bit excited, but he knew he must remind himself this wasn't a parade, but a war. This would be the moment of judgement to stand worthy as a mutant.

Ryan, however, didn't speak about it. He looked very passive, yet his expression felt strange, as if he was lost in his thoughts. Zenrot found it weird since Ryan was one of the most focused majors in Art Gun.

Finally, they reached the small vehicle and noticed soldiers were putting boxes on the passenger seat—meaning there wasn't enough space for Zenrot. He didn't mind though and told Ryan he'd jog to any destination he had to and help him deliver the supplies. It was an opportunity to prepare himself for the night. Ryan went to the driver's seat and started the cart, driving slow enough for Zenrot to easily keep pace. They made a few stops where the civilians slept, delivering boxes filled with clothes and enough supplies to survive for a few days until new merchandise arrived.

Ryan could see Zenrot's enthusiasm helping these people, and the courage to engage when some people were still afraid of mutants. It touched the major to know Zenrot was one of them, yet he still found a way to cheer them up and show there was a mutant who is willing to give anything for peace; to be accepted. Only few people could bring themselves to trust Zenrot's intentions, but it was enough for him. Ryan was very proud of the journey they had taken in training together, and of the man Zenrot had become—and for what was left to learn. It was almost getting dark by the time they had delivered all supplies. Ryan told Zenrot to sit on the passenger seat so he wouldn't need to jog for the rest of their journey. The cart started moving.

"Hey Ry—pardon me. Major." Zenrot quickly changed his mood to excitement again. "Permission to speak freely?"

"You don't need to ask permission to speak with me."

Zenrot flinched, then turned his head with an eyebrow raised. "Are you certain, major? Because last time I remember you told me to address you as 'sir' and to always ask for permission."

"That is correct." Ryan glanced at Zenrot then looked back to his driving. "It was more to learn some manners. Afterall, you were a stubborn man a few months back." Then he turns his head, smiling brightly to Zenrot. "Now you finally became a better living being."

"*Yeesh*. Thanks." Neither man could hold themselves back and both started laughing. After three months of cold training, it was the first time ever seeing Ryan truly having a sense of humor; to see him laugh and smile. "Now I can finally show I'm worthy to stand in the battlefield and fight."

Zenrot was speaking in a lively, excited way, but, Ryan's mood changed drastically back to his serious expression again at that comment. Zenrot started to wonder if he'd said anything wrong or something disrespectful.

Ryan looked ahead, concentrating on driving. "You don't need to be on the battlefield to prove you're worthy," he spoke flatly.

"What do you mean?" Zenrot didn't understand. In the distance he saw other groups of recruits drilling with their instructors as the cart drove closer to the training field. Zenrot was preparing himself mentally and physically to show his skills and to finally be sent outside to fight.

As they grew close to the training area, Ryan took a turn, driving away from the field. Zenrot was confused, and asked himself why Ryan was driving away. "Excuse me, major? We just missed the training field. Is there some urgency taking us away?"

No response from the major. He was focused on his driving.

They passed every building and tent on the way and, after several more minutes of driving, finally made a stop. They were at Zenrot's warehouse. He didn't understand why they had stopped at his barracks. "Did I miss anything? Do I need to pick up something before I start the trial?"

Still no response from Ryan. He put his hand on the cart's key and shut down the vehicle, then exhaled a long breath, finally turning to look at Zenrot.

"I'm afraid you won't be taking the trial," Ryan finally spoke. He was calm, but his voice lacked its usual certainty.

"Uh? Why not?" Zenrot asked, as confused as he could ever be. "We worked hard to finally achieve my physique in order for me to leave Art Gun and fight."

"I know, and you have done a great job. But... I think it's best if you stay here on Art Gun. To protect these people. You may never know when Sentry Run will invade here on our base."

"But you told me I was needed in the battle to fight. I'm to be with a team of mutants, right? So I won't be alone."

"Just because you'll fight with other mutants doesn't mean you can trust them."

"That doesn't make any sense. You said—"

"I know what I said before!" Ryan shouted angrily. Noticing the people around, watching them, he cleared his throat and visibly calmed himself to speak. "Look, outside these walls there is nothing but danger and cruelty. I can't afford to lose someone like you."

Zenrot felt dismayed at those words and clambered out of the cart. "Is it because I can be of use to you? Because of my abilities?" He was becoming agitated.

Ryan thought carefully about the words he chose. "I didn't mean it like that—"

"Then what did you really mean?" Zenrot interrupted. "Because the last time I checked you were assigned to train me to be a mutant soldier. To be part of a group called the MSF. It took three months... three months of endless workouts until I was ready. Not to mention that I was doing ridiculous exercises for a whole day at a time. And now you don't want me to fight?" Anger was apparent in Zenrot's tone, and his volume was slowly growing louder and louder; so loud that people around started to hear. Ryan noticed his body language, as well. His hands were turning into fists. People around started to get scared, and soldiers were keeping their eyes close on Zenrot.

"I understand you're angry," Ryan said gently to control the situation. "I'm just trying to look out for you. Please understand—"

"No! I don't understand at all!" Zenrot threw a punch at the side of the cart. Ryan immediately climbed out as the cart went sliding away and flipped to its side, falling to the ground. Every soldier aimed a weapon at Zenrot, ready to shoot him down.

"Wait!" Ryan screamed loudly. "Hold your fire!" He spoke to every soldier present with his hands in the air.

Zenrot reacted quickly and rushed to pull the cart back to its position. Fortunately, there was no one injured. He felt ashamed for how he had behaved. Zenrot looked around and saw people and soldiers alike were scared. Civilians quickly found cover in case danger happened, and the soldiers kept their aim on Zenrot. After Ryan's order, the civilians left their hideouts and awkwardly headed back on their routines. Soldiers lowered their rifles and walked away. The environment still felt tense. Ryan turned around, looking at Zenrot, who was now bowing his head.

"My sincere apologies, Major Ryan. Perhaps you're right." He walked to the door of the warehouse. "I must work on my anger, among other things, before I'm sent to battle. It is best if I just help at the base until it is really necessary for me to fight." Just before he was about to enter the warehouse, a bunch of the other recruits got in the way and walked inside of the building first. Zenrot stood outside, in front of the door, looking spacey and onto the ground. After a moment, he gazed at Ryan. "Once again, I'm very sorry for what I did."

Zenrot opened the door and walked inside the warehouse. The soldiers inside were talking with each other. Some were sitting on their bunk beds while others were standing. When they noticed Zenrot walk in, everyone stared at him; they were watching him like a threat after his behavior with Ryan.

Zenrot walked to his bed where there were new clothes for sleep. Everyone sat in awkward silence, viewing him without even blinking. Some roommates even chuckled. Zenrot could hear them talking about how he would never succeed as a mutant soldier, how he would never leave these walls because he looked dangerous to work with.

Zenrot simply ignored them and headed to the bathroom.

It was a simple, functional room. The far side of the room held a row of showers, each separated by a short wall and with a curtain for privacy. As he headed for one of the shower stalls, he passed sinks and mirrors on his right and a row of toilets along the wall to his left. He undressed and tossed his dirty clothes in to the large, communal bin in the center of the room before turning on the water and methodically scrubbing himself clean. The heat from the water was soothing, and he soon found his mind wandering back to the major.

The fear on the face of the people who had witnessed his outburst was seared into his mind's eye. He brushed his teeth while under the steaming shower to save time and to try and push off the negative feelings threatening to overwhelm him. Guilt sat heavy in his stomach as well—after weeks of hard work to prove his good intentions with the community he had sunk everything in one moment of poor self-control.

He sighed, turning off the water and rubbing himself dry with the thin, military-issue towel. What's done was done. He grabbed his kit and, in pajamas, returned to the bunkroom.

Walking outside the bathroom, he saw most people sleeping in their bunk beds. Few of them were still awake, though some were still laying in their beds hoping to fall asleep soon. Others were still standing around, talking to each other. Unfortunately, the ones standing were next to Zenrot's bunk. This could be some trouble, Zenrot realized as he walked to his bed and moved his sheet to get comfortable. Two of his roommates walked towards him, standing behind as he prepared his bed. He noticed it wasn't a friendly-feeling approach.

"So…" said one of them. "How does it feel being rejected to work as a soldier?"

"I know why," said the other roommate as he softly smacks his chest for attention. "Because a mutant isn't supposed to be a soldier of Art Gun."

"If he was a decent mutant, he wouldn't be here with us. He's just a boy with weird eyes. I don't know why they bothered to train *you*—" He leveled a glare at Zenrot. "—when you're just a waste of time."

"That's funny," Zenrot answered, turning around to face them. "Coming from two recruits who failed the test many times, I mean. In any case, the one who shouldn't be here is you guys." Both recruits were shocked, fury on their faces at Zenrot answering back.

"Did he just—"

"Yes, he did." The other recruit spoke softly, yet in anger. He started cracking his knuckles. "I guess I have to teach this boy a lesson to respect his elders." Other recruits start raising up from their beds; about ten of them stood, ready to take on Zenrot. It wouldn't be a difficult fight considering he has immense strength, but if he made another bad move and attacked one of his teammates it wouldn't go in his favor. People had already started judging him. Moments earlier soldiers had been ready to shoot him for attacking Ryan by accident because of his emotions. If he dropped his behavior to their level, *that* would be voluntary.

Zenrot closed his eyes, lowered his head, and sighed. Then he looked up to the recruits. "If you do this, all of you will be expelled for fighting against a mutant and basically going against the exact thing that Art Gun is trying to achieve." He hoped that would scare them into standing down, but it didn't.

"You think that is going to stop us? Besides, you just acted aggressively against an officer. We're almost ten people against you. Who do you think Art Gun will vouch for? You? Or us?" The recruit kept coming closer and closer. Zenrot was holding his fist and trying his best not to attack. If they start a fight, however, he would have no choice. He must fight. "I'm going to enjoy this," the recruit whispered while raising his right arm, ready to swing his first punch.

Zenrot raised his arm to defend himself, but the fist never came. Something crashed from the roof—an indistinct form stomping on the recruit and squeezing him into pieces. An invader with a shield on his left arm pushed Zenrot a few feet away, making him crash into a few bunk beds.

"Help! We are being attacked!" another recruit shouted. "Everyone get the hell out of— *ugh!*" The recruit stopped speaking and started drooling blood from his mouth. He slowly looked down to his chest in disbelief. He was being stabbed with a spear and slowly lifted into the air. After a moment, he was thrown away like nothing. Everyone else was running, panicked, and leaving the warehouse. Zenrot slowly stood, looking at the attacker.

"ALERT... DETECTING MUTANT NEARBY..." It was a robot. When it turned around to face Zenrot, it didn't look like the Golem back in the city of Scatenor, but it did have Sentry Run's colors as a design, blue and orange with white strokes, on the arms. The robot was huge, about two feet taller than Zenrot, and solid metal. There were no cables showing or obvious weak spot Zenrot could easily attack. Sentry Run had been busy, making sure the robots were more protected from incoming damage. His head was shaped like a medieval helmet, and its eyes shone as a straight, horizontal, blue neon line—a sensor to detect the enemy. This robot had a spear in his right hand and a shield on the left hand; except that the shield *was* its hand, then it transformed into an ordinary hand with bold metal fingers. By the looks of it, it was the robot mentioned months ago by Ryan when Art Gun brought metal pieces in to examinate them— a Spartan.

"MUTANT SIGHTED..." The robot charged to attack by stabbing Zenrot with the spear. He snatched a mattress from the metal frame and swung with it to hit the spear away, then went for a punch to break the right arm. The Spartan robot reacted quickly, turning its left hand to a shield and hitting Zenrot directly. The force pushed him away until he bounced against a wall, leaving cracks where he landed. Zenrot painfully stood, grinding his teeth at the discomfort in his back.

The Spartan rushed forward with the spear leveled and the shield covering itself. Zenrot raised both of his fists, waiting for it to come closer. When the Spartan got close enough, Zenrot dodged to the right side. He grabbed the spear with his left hand and immediately punched directly to the shield, knocking the robot into the air where it broke through a wall, falling outside the warehouse. Zenrot rushed to the Spartan, jumping and landing on top of the robot before it could recover. With both hands, he grabbed the shield attached to its hand and smashed the Spartan's head with it several times in succession. Tossing the shield away, he followed up by punching directly into the Spartan's chest, breaking right through the armored plating there. He wrapped his hands around as many cables as he could and yanked them out, making sure it was destroyed for good.

Zenrot was breathing heavily and agitated. He had been so focused on the fight that when he looked up, he was surprised to see the soldiers with guns and cars with machine guns mounted on them all aiming at the Spartan. Shock was clear on everyone's face—he'd defeated a Spartan with his bare hands. Zenrot climbed off the Spartan and walked away. Half of the soldiers pointed their weapons at Zenrot, while the other half were still aiming at the Spartan.

"I can't tell—" he said, raising his voice but not turning to address the soldiers, "—does the fact that I crushed that Spartan make you happy or scared?"

CHAPTER FIVE

Zenrot was in his pajamas and being escorted by a soldier. They were heading to Art Gun's main building to meet up with Arashi and walking in an awkward silence. Zenrot wondered what was going to happen since the invasion.

"Am I in trouble?" he asked out of curiosity, but the soldier didn't respond or even look at him, keeping his distance until they arrived at the office. They entered the main building. Scientists and soldiers roamed around in panic, but it didn't look as crowded as when Zenrot had arrived that first day.

At a distance, Mojo and some of his assistants were working with gadgets and devices for the army. He was working desperately, pushing his workers for results. Glancing up, his eyes came to rest on Zenrot being escorted toward Arashi's office.

Mojo dropped what he was working on and ran to Zenrot. "Hello there!" He stopped them from proceeding by standing directly in the path. The man was soaked with sweat and had soggy, drowsy eyes. Zenrot could tell he'd been working for many hours straight. Mojo stretched his hand to introduce himself. "My name is Mojo Denavor, Director of the Science and Research Unit in Art Gun."

Zenrot stretched his hand out to shake Mojo's. "I'm Zenrot." The handshake was mistimed, and the scientist held his limply; it was awkward.

"Interesting..." Mojo said while letting go of Zenrot's hand and examining him from different angles. "Do you have a last name?"

"If I do... I don't remember, sir."

"Ah, an educated child," Mojo nearly purred. He sounded very pleased.

"You can thank Major Ryan."

"Well, if you don't remember your last name, you can choose your own..." He turned around and lifted Zenrot's arm, looked at his legs, and examined his eyes closely. "Since there is no record of your former past and you can't remember anything, you can start making a new one to start fresh." He took a few steps away, still looking at Zenrot. "I must be going. I have to work on new defense systems now that the robots have managed to invade our base. I'm looking forward to working with you. I'll see you soon," he said, before running back to work, yelling at his assistants to work faster on the way.

"Let's keep going," the soldier said flatly as they continued walking.

"Right..." Zenrot followed to the elevator, glancing over his shoulder and thinking about Mojo. *What a weird guy.* They reached Arashi's floor and could immediately hear the screaming in the room before the doors even opened. Everyone was arguing about how the robots had invaded inside the Art Gun compound without anyone noticing. Voices were angry in pointing out how many people died during the invasion and, from what Zenrot was hearing, that it was mostly mutants targeted. Arashi was sitting on his desk, discussing with another soldier. To Zenrot's surprise, Ryan was standing quietly at his right.

"How many did we lose?" Arashi asked.

"A lot," the soldier answered. "Five Spartan robots invaded and attacked most of the mutants around base. Astred took out three of them. A coordinated group of soldiers took out one, and the last one—well…"

"The last one is eliminated," the soldier escorting Zenrot interrupted. "This mutant killed the Spartan with his bare hands."

"Ah, you're finally here!" Arashi sounded excited. He looked at the soldier and said, "You can leave now!" The soldier nodded and walked away.

Zenrot was left alone and fearfully looked at Arashi. "Am I in trouble, sir?" he asked through his teeth.

"Not at all, my child." He stood up in his excitement. "I must say, I'm very impressed with your performance. It takes courage and efficiency to defeat a Spartan." Arashi gazed at Ryan. "Some doubted you from the very start." Ryan stood at attention, yet he lowered his head as Arashi looked back at Zenrot. "It was only a matter of time until you finally discovered your true potential." Arashi stepped to Zenrot, slowly walking around him, before resting his arm on Zenrot's shoulder and guiding him to walk toward the giant windows.

"You see," the general continued, "I gave you special training to prepare you because I knew that, someday, you'd be a fine candidate for the Mutant Special Force." They reached the window and Arashi put his hands over Zenrot's shoulders. He leaned forward, whispering into his ear. "From this day forward, you are an official member of the MSF." Zenrot gasped, surprised at the news. An official soldier to fight for Art Gun.

Arashi walked towards his desk. "Starting tomorrow you will be assigned officially to the MSF. You won't be staying in the warehouse anymore. Sentry Run sent their robots and I will need my strongest mutants together in case this happens again. Besides, I can't let any soldier—or anyone else, for that matter—mistreat the ones who represent what we're fighting to protect. You will be staying in a private building, one only for the MSF to stay in. Each mutant will have their own room."

Everything Arashi said sounded too great to not be excited about, yet Zenrot felt there was a catch tied to all these rewards for the mutants. He turned from the window and walked slowly to Arashi. "I assume I'll have special training as well?" Zenrot guessed, stopping a few feet away from Arashi's desk.

"That is correct." Arashi sat back down at his desk. "Aside from the super strength, based on the information Ryan gave me and today's action... we acknowledge that you have a certain style when it comes to a fight." Four people arrived from the elevator. They formed one line standing next to each other. Each wore a unique uniform decorated with a variety of different badges.

"Who are they?" Zenrot asked curiously.

Arashi ordered the majors to introduce themselves and the first stepped forward. She was broad faced, with similar short, spiked hair to Zenrot's own. She nodded brusquely, and began to list a variety of foreign sounding nonsense words that he took were different styles of martial arts she was an apparent expert in. She motioned to the elaborate looking pistols strapped to her thigh and promised that she could turn him into a true marksman.

The next man stepped forward with precision as she stepped back into line. He was tall and lanky, but wiry with muscle. He began to describe the encyclopedic knowledge he had of historic wars, strategy, and tactics, and it took Zenrot a moment to realize that knives seemed to be appearing and disappearing from his hands as he spoke. The major was flawlessly producing and re-hiding different blades through what looked to be sleight of hand. As he finished his minute-long sales pitch, he casually slipped the last knife into his belt and winked.

The third major stepped forward while the other man stepped back in line. She was short with her hair in a high bun and explained how she specialized in demolitions and using equipment and surroundings to take advantage in a fight. She took out an explosive device and explained how efficient it was to use as either a distraction or an opportunity to use against an enemy. She also explained how to craft small explosives. Zenrot felt it was way too much information compared to just engaging an enemy.

Lastly, the fourth major stepped forward as the short officer stepped back. He was half-again shorter than the others and built like a bulldog. He announced that he specialized in combat support, gesturing to his many medals symbolizing expertise in chemical warfare, combat engineering, communications and so on. He explained how he used each role to support his fellow troops, and that he also knows every tactic to fight against an enemy for those in need. Zenrot noticed that this Major focus on the many subjects to be best prepared in a war. After the major stopped speaking, he nodded his head and stepped back.

They all sounded very confident, very professional. But Zenrot was at a loss for words. He wondered to himself what he could possibly ask to these majors. He had no legitimate questions because, deep down, he didn't trust them. It wasn't because they wouldn't do well at their job, but because of what Mr. Han had said about the majors in general. Most would train poorly and send Zenrot to battle without proper preparation. Judging by how some soldiers had looked at Zenrot with despair and how the recruits back at the warehouse tried to get him in trouble, it was clear that he couldn't simply trust anyone. Despite everything that had occurred against Zenrot and the struggles along the way, there *was* someone he still trusted. He glanced at Ryan and noticed he was standing like a stone; he still hadn't spoken since Zenrot had arrived. He turned to look at the other majors, then turned on his heel to face Arashi.

"May I ask one request, General Arashi?" Zenrot asked politely.

"Of course, name it."

"You said I could choose anyone, right...?" He looked back at Ryan, then to Arashi again. "I was wondering if I could choose Major Ryan Venango." They were all surprised by his request.

Ryan raised his head in shock and Arashi turned his head to look at Zenrot, eyes opened wide. "I started my training with Major Ryan, might as well finish with him. If that's all right with you, sir." Zenrot stood rigid in front of Arashi's desk.

"Are you sure, Zenrot?" Arashi asked. "Any of these majors is capable of giving you the best training experience to develop into the best mutant you can be. Ryan, however…" His eyes flitted to Ryan then back to Zenrot. "He hasn't had any experience training mutants for the battlefield. I did tell him to train you at MSF level, but that was only to be physically prepared." He leaned on his desk with his hands held together, moving close to Zenrot. "This is now for the warzone," he said in a deep voice. It was a sign to remember this wasn't a walk through the base any longer—now came the real threat. "You understand where I'm going with this, right?"

"I understand," Zenrot answered, taking careful steps away from the desk. "But my reason for choosing Major Ryan is because he has made me who I am today. Without his proper training, I may have not survived the fight with the Spartan." He turned his eyes to Ryan with a smile on his face. "I believe he will be the right mentor for the job," Zenrot said confidently.

Arashi looked seriously to Ryan and asked if he could take the responsibility of training him well enough as a mutant. The major said it would be an honor for him to train Zenrot and acknowledged that he had to be very careful because failing was not an option.

"You have exactly a month," Arashi threatened. "Regardless of his condition, you have one month to get him ready. Same goes for the other mutants chosen to be an MSF soldier." Arashi shuffled through his files and handed Ryan a letter. "Here's a list of events that Zenrot must complete during the month while you train him. I expect good results." Arashi raised his hand and snapped his fingers. One of his bodyguards appeared behind Zenrot and Ryan like a shadow; both of whom were startled. "He will escort you to the building assigned to the mutants only. Zenrot's room will be number four. I'll be busy assigning more soldiers to defend inside the base, then I'll take some rest. Be on your guard, gentlemen. Dismissed." Both saluted and turned to follow Arashi's bodyguard on their way to Zenrot's new lodging.

***

Zenrot and Ryan finally reached where members of the MSF were going to stay for the rest of the war. It was a building two stories high with black walls, a red design, and an elaborate entrance door made of glass. Above the door there was a motion sensor. Ryan took the first step in front of the door, and it slid open automatically. Inside there was a huge hallway with three doors each on the left and right side. At the end of the hallway, there was a staircase that led to the second floor. As Ryan continued forward, Zenrot followed.

None of them had spoken on their way to the building, but Ryan finally broke the silence. "Well, here we are." They had reached the door with a "04" number plate attached. He opened the interior door and signaled with his hand for Zenrot to enter first. Stepping in, he noted that it was completely different and way safer compared to the warehouse. It was a small room, but it had some fine decorations: a square red carpet in the center, wall sconces, and a full-size bed with gray sheets. Zenrot turned around, noticing a cabinet. Opening it, he saw a new uniform and new clothes for the night. There was also another door and, upon opening it, he realized he now had a private bathroom.

"This is definitely better than the warehouse…" Zenrot said as he walked around admiring the place. "All this for an MSF member?"

Ryan gave a short smile at seeing how enthusiastic he looked about the room. "That's right. Arashi wants to make sure that all the members of the MSF are treated well enough, so they feel safe." Then his mood turned serious. "After all, those are the ones who are going to be on the front lines. Congratulations on your promotion," he added lightly.

Zenrot had a feeling Ryan wasn't overly happy that he was now an official soldier. A couple of hours ago things had gotten heated because Ryan wanted him to stay on base and protect it, which had made Zenrot furious. That felt very awkward in retrospect since Zenrot had chosen him as his trainer once again. There was no turning back, yet he still didn't want things to be uncomfortable between them.

"You don't sound very convincing," Zenrot pointed out.

"I am. It's just… never mind." Ryan gave a pause, and Zenrot could recognize he wanted to say something, yet was struggling not to speak about it. "Better get some rest," he changed the subject, "because tomorrow we'll start our new training at—"

"5:00 a.m.?" Zenrot interrupted with a smirk on his face.

Ryan laughed softly. "Correct. Expect an extreme workout

this time, along with Arashi's objectives. This won't be easy."

"I'm up for the challenge." He returned a smile back to Ryan with real enthusiasm.

"All right, I'll leave you to it." Ryan walked nearly out of the room and stopped. "I must ask you something, though… why you chose me to be your trainer?"

"Honestly, because I can trust you." He lowered his gaze, trying not to look at him as he nervously continued. "Despite the hard work you made me go through and our little discussion… You haven't given up on me, and that's something I haven't seen from anyone else." Zenrot felt cliché speaking his thoughts out loud, but the admission still somehow made him smile.

"Good night, soldier." Ryan gave his last words gently as he closed the door. Zenrot jumped into his bed, facing up at the ceiling. He was tired from everything that had happened that day. Had he been imagining that things had gotten better between him and Ryan? The major's smirks and that look like he'd felt flattered made Zenrot think things may have been solved. It wasn't a direct answer, but it would suffice. Thinking deeply about the situation, his eyes grew lazy, then slowly closed as a deep sleep claimed him.

CHAPTER SIX

There were only five minutes left until 4:30 a.m. Zenrot had been awake since three o'clock in the morning, anxious and only having had four hours of sleep. He had taken a long shower and dressed in his new uniform, but had spent the rest of the time sitting on the side of his bed waiting to head out to the field. He was trying to maintain focus for any challenges which may occur. It wasn't about basic training for a perfect soldier; it was about being one of the best mutants for Art Gun. Yet there was something that had been bothering him.

Zenrot thought about what could have happened before he was found by Art Gun. He tried his best to remember if he had family or even friends to recall in his memories. Instead, only war and destruction. All he knew about himself was that he has super strength, but there must be something else… something more inside himself. For all his trying, however, Zenrot still struggled the more he thought about it. There was also something else upsetting him.

The recruit back on his first day of training had mentioned two mutants who had caused this war to happen. One had vaporized an entire zone full of people, and another one had massacred the audience of a circus show. Zenrot wondered what had happened to those mutants after their attacks. Surely, there must be *some* actions to prevent this from happening ever again, but declaring war and eliminating every mutant in existence was going too far. Not all mutants were capable of such cruelty such as the two who had started this mess. Zenrot, at least, knew that he didn't believe in ever committing such horrendous acts. Sure, he was at war, but so far he had only destroyed robots. Zenrot only hoped not to have to cross the line to kill a living being.

Zenrot looked at the clock—exactly 4:30 a.m. He stood up and walked towards the door, the movement beginning to soothe his nerves. Opening the door, a letter was stuck on the outside of his room. He pulled the letter down and opened it. It had a message that read:

Morning Zenrot, we won't be meeting in the field today. Meet me at Art Gun's main gate. Don't be late, or you will be punished... Not just with running through base this time.
-Ryan

"Does he ever sleep?" Zenrot said in amazement. He left his room and closed the door, beginning the walk to the entrance gate. The security checkpoint was on high alert, with tanks periodically driving by with soldiers on top holding the vehicle-mounted machine guns. Other soldiers marched around with guns in their hands, wearing new gray and silver bullet-proof vests. They looked to be designed by Mojo and his team, yet still wouldn't be enough against Sentry Run's robots. They needed to invent something greater, and fast.

Zenrot could feel that he was being stared at as he walked. He could hear soldiers whispering with each other after the incident in the warehouse and see that they despised him when he caught their eye. He couldn't tell if they were relieved or scared at how he had destroyed the Spartan. Zenrot turned his head, looking straight at the gate. He could see Ryan standing in the distance in a comfortable uniform and a military backpack; he looked ready to travel.

Zenrot reached the gate. "Good morning, Major Ryan."

He looks at his watch on his left wrist. "It's 4:50 a.m.," he said flatly.

Zenrot was confused. "Aren't we supposed to reunite for training at 5:00 a.m.?"

"You're ten minutes early."

"I mean, is that a bad thing?"

"You need to be at least twenty-to-thirty minutes early to be considered *early*," Ryan clarified. "It's important to be strict with our time to execute any plan accordingly."

"I mean... it's still early..."

Ryan nodded his head once. "Let's go." He once again spoke flatly as he started walking.

"Geez... And I thought I needed some manners," Zenrot said in a low volume so the major wouldn't hear.

"What did you say?" Ryan asked, glancing back over his

shoulder.

"Nothing!" he said, scared. Zenrot kept following without another word.

Both started walking outside the base on a path filled with dirt, with small rocks and trees on the sides. As they followed the track, trucks passed by on their way to the battlefield. Ryan made a turn and walked between the trees, and Zenrot questioned where exactly he was planning to go. He could hear gunshots and explosions in the distance, though luckily far enough away for anyone to notice them. After almost an hour of walking with no conversation with one another, he was thirsty for water, but didn't dare to ask Ryan if he had brought some. Up ahead there were many rocks and large boulders. The boulders were huge, easily as tall as a twenty-story building. It looked like it was clear of danger.

"All right, we're here," Ryan finally said.

Zenrot crouched, putting his hands on his knees to breathe. "About time," he said in relief at his diminishing pain. He was drenched with sweat from the long walk.

Ryan examined the area while Zenrot caught his breath. He found an enormous boulder almost a hundred feet tall and called for Zenrot. The major told him that he must climb all the way to the top without any equipment. At first, Zenrot thought he was joking, but that thought quickly faded as he saw Ryan was as serious as he had ever been. Ryan explained this particular training was to prepare Zenrot for any difficult situation that may present itself during the war. Ryan waited in a shady spot while watching him climb.

"Make sure you don't fall," he called up with his usual even tone of voice. Zenrot was approaching the boulder while looking up and couldn't see the end of it. He searched for a location where it was comfortable to climb, and finally found a ledge that seemed like it might work. He started climbing.

"Take all the time you need," Ryan said calmly. Zenrot gazed down at him, then looked back up, focusing on climbing cautiously. Each step required searching for where he could grab tightly to pull himself up. Step by step, he was going higher and higher. He grabbed a tiny hole to help himself push, but the rock crumbled underneath his grip. Zenrot lost control and fell all the way down, landing flat against the ground.

"Augh! Damn it!" he shouted in pain, quickly standing up. He looked at Ryan, sitting on a rock watching everything. "That hurt! Do I really have to get to the top?" He was furious.

Ryan nodded, looking towards the giant boulder. Then, dryly, "Again."

"Can't I at least have some equipment or something to protect me from a high fall?"

"Nope!"

"What if my back would have broken? Or worse?" he asked, agitated.

"You're a mutant. Most mutants can handle up to three times more physical pain than a human."

"You said most mutants!" Zenrot clarified. "What if I was the exception and couldn't withstand that type of physical pain?"

"Then your spine would have broken when that robot used you to crack the wall of the warehouse you used to sleep in,"

Ryan said without hesitation. Zenrot was starting to think it had been a mistake to choose him as a trainer once again. "So, again," he insisted, raising his voice.

Zenrot started climbing. He made it a few inches higher than his first try but fell again near the same point. He stood slowly and looked over his shoulder at Ryan, still peacefully waiting for results. He tried many more times over the next two hours—over and over—and ended up with many bruises from hitting the ground countless times.

As Zenrot stood from his latest failure, Ryan walked past him. "That's enough for today. We'll go on to another training event," he said, heading in another direction. Zenrot was so happy to hear that. A few minutes away, the ground was so cracked he could see thirty feet all the way down. "All right, here's what you're going to do," Ryan started explaining, "we know you have strength, but I need you to demonstrate speed. Run as fast as you can until the end of the road, where the soil is no longer destroyed." The area in front of them had small squares of soil atop the pieces of fractured ground. Each had a width of one to two feet, but the gap between the makeshift, natural platforms was closer to eight or ten yards. Not only was he being asked to run fast but jump high as well. His goal was nearly fifty yards away.

"Your goal is to finish in one minute," Ryan intoned.

"To reach to the other side?"

"No, to reach the other side and get back here. One minute."

Zenrot was shocked. "You must be joking!" His voice reached a high pitch. "That's inhuman!"

"It is a little inhuman," he said sarcastically. He then looked straight at Zenrot and said seriously, without hesitation, "but not impossible for a mutant like you. So… I want that done in a minute. There," he pointed to where Zenrot needed to reach, "and here." The spot where they were standing. "If you fall, you must come back and start again. Let's get set." He told him to get into position to run. Zenrot crouched with his hands touching the floor, one leg stretched behind him, and the other bent underneath his torso. Ryan stood with a hand in the air.

"Ready… set… go!"

Ryan threw his arm down and Zenrot started running and jumping as fast as he could from one piece of ground to the next to try and reach his destination. With one jump, he landed clumsily at the edge of the platform. He slipped, trying to grab onto something, but had no luck. He fell all the way down in the crevasse, landing on his feet thirty feet down. He was impressed his legs weren't crushed at the landing—in fact, Zenrot didn't feel much pain at all; only a minor ache that disappeared in a minute.

He returned to Ryan and saw that the major didn't look surprised. "Do you realize what just happened?" Zenrot yelled, enthusiasm coming from his own surprise, once he got close.

"That you failed?" Ryan responded dryly.

"Are you kidding me?" he said with amazement, aiming both arms to where he had fallen. "I fell almost thirty feet deep. How are my legs not in pain or even crushed?" He flailed his arms, gesturing at Ryan. "Aren't you even considering the situation right now?"

"I am. I was expecting that." Zenrot was confused and had

other questions forming. Ryan noticed his expression and continued explaining. "You've already proven you have immense strength, which means your body, especially your muscles, can handle heavy strain—meaning landing from a tall height as well. However, you may experience cramps and discomfort a bit."

Ryan sat down, opened his backpack, withdrew a notebook, and recorded notes on Zenrot's progress. "I'm a hundred percent sure—" He continued writing in his notebook as he spoke. "—you have more to offer than super strength. It would be a lot easier if I knew anything about you. Unfortunately, you have no memories of that." Zenrot lowered his head feeling regret at his memory loss. "So, I'll find it out my way." Ryan closed his notebook and looked at him. "As I said before, most mutants I've seen have not double, but triple resistance in their body. Some have specializations in strength, speed, knowledge, or other skills. It all depends on their abilities, of course, not just the basics of being a mutant."

"And you're willing to do whatever it takes, even if it costs my life?" Zenrot mumbled as he looked up at Ryan.

"One thing I learned from mutants. They *do* whatever it takes to survive in a dangerous situation." He stood up and pointed toward the crumbling ground. "Come on, again."

Zenrot tried over and over, making some forward progress as he tried variations in his jumps or route, but ultimately continuing to fall. As with much of his training so far, as the hours passed everything became more difficult. This time, far beyond where it had when he trained back at the base; none of what had come before compared to lifting many heavy boulders—some triple the size of Zenrot!—or running up impossibly high walls. But even these two feats were not all Ryan needed him to accomplish.

The two men were walking near an area filled with a strange mist. Ryan told him to be very careful not to breathe while inside the mist, because it was radioactive, and if he breathed it long enough it would burn his throat—severely enough to make a hole through his neck and cause many other equally unpleasant symptoms. It was training to survive being confronted with a wide category of complex attacks: chemical weapons, biological agents, radioactive materials, actual nuclear weapons, or high-yield explosives. There was an acronym for all these nasty situations, and Ryan told him that even this CBRNE training was special.

Normally, soldiers had a gas mask for these situations. For Zenrot it was totally different: he must walk through with minimum breathing until the time was up and then come back. This event was a special request from Arashi, and Ryan explained that it was an exercise for him to experience different symptoms and how to embrace—and ultimately work through—them in battle.

"There will be a point when the symptoms are too strong and you will want to get some fresh air," the major warned, "but you must hold your breath until the time is done." Zenrot asked how long he needed to hold his breath while under the mist and casually held up an open hand, all fingers splayed. Five minutes. He was not allowed to leave the mist until ordered to evacuate the area. "Are you ready?" Ryan asked.

"Can I have a moment to think this through?" he asked nervously.

"No. Ready... Set..." Ryan shouted, and Zenrot got into position. "Go!"

Zenrot ran deep into the mist. He stopped and walked around to look at the area around him. Gray mist, nothing to see. *Only have to stay in for five minutes. This should be easy.* Zenrot stood like a stone, glancing around to distract himself from the idea of time passing. Almost a minute had passed when he started to feel stranger by the second. His eyes were full of tears, and he found himself rubbing his arm across his face to clean them. Feeling dizzy, hallucinating, and with an itching throat, Zenrot tried to take a step. He almost fell. He carefully began touching himself all around his body, feeling as if something was burning his skin. His eyes were all watery once again, and boogers were running out of his nose. His lips were tight and painfully swollen.

He slowly walked in the direction he had come from; with all the mist he could barely see a way out. "Major Ryan..." he gasped in a soft tone, struggling to talk. "Is it... time?" He took another step and fell to his knees, dragging himself out of the mist. He wanted to close his eyes, just to see if the pain would go away. Minutes felt like hours with all the pain and symptoms wracking his body. Just when he was about to close his eyes and stop struggling, he heard a voice far away.

"Zenrot..." He heard an echo. "Zenrot... Zen... Zenrot!" Ryan was shouting louder and louder.

Zenrot came back to his senses.

"It has been more than five minutes! Get out of there!"

He stood up, pulling himself together, and sprinted toward a light in the distance. He was moving away from the mist. Running and running and finally—the sun was out.

Zenrot was breathing heavily, but he had made it out. He threw himself to the ground to rest and inhale and exhale slowly. Ryan tossed his backpack aside and rushed to check on him. "Are you all right?"

"How long... was I in there?" He was still breathing heavily as he spoke.

"For almost ten minutes," the major answered worriedly.

He laughed softly and, with returning confidence, said, "I broke the record, right?"

"You almost killed yourself in there!" Ryan shouted with genuine anger. "I told you to breathe slowly and to concentrate."

"But I survived—"

"That is not surviving! That was luck!" he interrupted, then kept yelling at Zenrot. "I thought I had to go pick you up. If you focused enough this wouldn't have happened." He handed Zenrot some water to help his recovery and gave him five minutes to rest.

"I thought I did—" Zenrot tried to express himself while Ryan walked to his backpack and stalked away, leaving Zenrot alone to rest.

Zenrot felt bad because he had sincerely believed he succeeded the five-minute challenge under the mist. He'd believed Ryan would be proud, but all he received was disappointment. Deep down, he knew Ryan was right—it was pure luck that he had survived. A few more seconds more in the mist and he would have been dead for sure.

When Zenrot finally recovered, he went to Ryan. It was getting hotter with the sun aiming directly at them. He was sweating all over, as wet as if he had been in the bath with clothes on. He was thirsty and starving; he hadn't eaten since he woke up.

Zenrot noticed a lake near where Ryan was waiting. Looking at the water, he couldn't see where it ended. It was so deep as to seem bottomless. Ryan took a length of rope out of his backpack, handed it to Zenrot, and told him to tie it to the heaviest rock he could find. He had to dive in the lake while holding the rock and remain underwater.

Then Ryan added, "Remember, your goal is to hold your breath underwater for," he hesitated a moment, then added, "ten minutes." He paused, giving Zenrot a pointed look, but the younger man didn't catch the glance or the increase in the length of time. "On this exercise, I don't expect you to do well today. I'll always be taking your time. If you reach at least thirty seconds, that's a start. After that your goal is to reach a minute, then you keep breaking your time after that. If you do less than what you've previously achieved, you will be doing community service with me in Art Gun for the rest of the night. Any questions?"

"Is it too late to ask for another trainer?" Zenrot said sarcastically.

Ryan glared and pushed Zenrot toward the lake. He grabbed the rope, tied it to the giant rock, and brought it along with him deep into the water. Settling into the lake, the giant rock loomed next to him, sinking beneath the water. Then the rock pulled

Zenrot deeper. He tried to stop from going down by pulling the rope, but it was very heavy—especially underwater. Zenrot held his breath the best he could, trying to swim his way up, but failing. The rock kept pulling him down.

He finally reached the bottom of the lake. In the darkness, Zenrot was left standing next to the rock. He swam back up, trying to lift it by holding the rope with one hand and swimming with the other. The boulder was too heavy, and he didn't even manage to lift it from the ground. Hitting the point where he couldn't hold his breath any longer, he let go of the rope and powered himself to the surface to get some fresh air, swimming faster and faster until he finally made it out.

Sucking in deep breaths, Zenrot turned to look at Ryan with visible frustration. "Sir, with all due respect… that's impossible to lift underwater. It's two times— three times the weight of pulling a boulder that size outside the water!"

Ryan was looking at his watch, noting the time, then looked at Zenrot floating in the water. "Thirty-two seconds… You can do more than that."

"Are you even listening?" Zenrot angrily shouted.

"*Mph?* Oh yes, you left your rock at the bottom of the river."

"It's heavy as fuck!" Zenrot yelled over him.

"Did you just swear in front of me, soldier?"

"My apologies, sir," Zenrot muttered as he swam to the shore.

"Where are you going?" the major shouted and pointed downward. "Get back there and pick up your rock."

Zenrot rolls his eyes, took a deep breath, and dove back

down to try again, holding his breath this time. Sometimes he held his breath for more than thirty seconds... sometimes less. He couldn't lift the rock even an inch from the ground, however. He tried, over and over, for more than an hour before Ryan grew irritated and ordered Zenrot to conclude this training for today. His next training would be back in the base.

Ryan walked peacefully on their way back, carrying his backpack. Meanwhile, Zenrot's legs were shaking, and he was barely able to walk in a straight line. As they walked, Ryan explained that these new training events must be finished, and that they wouldn't rest until Zenrot achieved every single one of them.

Deep down Ryan was very worried, thinking of what Arashi had warned him. *Get Zenrot trained in exactly a month.* If he kept on like he had today, it would probably take more than a month to get to where Zenrot needed to be, but he couldn't afford to fail... not now. Arashi was already mad that Ryan had tried to convince him to keep Zenrot inside Art Gun; if he failed to train him, there would be dire consequences. Not only for him, but for Zenrot as well.

At two in the afternoon, and back on the Art Gun base, Zenrot was feeling relieved. The morning of training and subsequent walk back had been hard, but he was finally going to get to eat. Ryan noticed his excitement, then casually warned Zenrot that he wouldn't be eating until he finished one last training event. They walked into a local establishment on the compound; it was a small gym. There were punching bags, ropes, and dumbbells all over the place. At the end of the gym, there was a squared boxing ring with three ropes attached to a metal pole in each corner surrounding it.

"Why are we here?" Zenrot asked.

"I'm going to teach you how to fight properly." He laid his backpack next to the ring and took off his uniform shirt.

"All right, so who is going to teach me that?"

"I am." He wore a gray undershirt and was wrapping bandages around his knuckles.

"You're joking, right? Do you remember what I did to the Spartan?"

"Do you remember who beat you? Hand to hand?" Zenrot felt a rush of shame and looked away. Ryan chuckled, then climbed inside the ring and stretched his arms and legs. "This is about surviving in case you're out of energy."

"Energy?" Zenrot got curious.

"You may have your strength—and probably other abilities—but if you exceed your limits, you may experience exhaustion and find it hard to focus on your opponent during battle. That will make you vulnerable." Ryan nodded and, with his finger, signaled to Zenrot to move closer. "So, if one day you find you can't use your abilities in battle, you can still defend yourself with martial arts and other tricks. Before we start on this training, though, you'll need to promise that under no circumstances will you use your true strength against me."

"Afraid?" Zenrot glared at him with a sharp smile as he approached.

"No," he said bluntly. "You need to learn to defend yourself without your abilities, just like we must defend ourselves sometimes without any weapons. People can be confident with a gun in their hands, but not many are without one." His body flowed into a combat position. "So, let's get started." Zenrot stood in what he felt like was his fighting position—Ryan could tell by his posture that it was going to take a while.

Taking their time, Ryan showed Zenrot every defensive technique he would need in case it came to hand-to-hand combat. He demonstrated throwing punches, kicks, and using quick reflexes. As Zenrot carefully learned each move, he fought one versus one against Ryan—and unfortunately lost every match. Every time he fell to the ground, Ryan offered his hand to help him stand.

"Never underestimate an opponent, even if they look easy to defeat. Again." They kept practicing over and over, but Zenrot keeps failing, again and again. He was getting frustrated and wanted to lean on his strength to win, but he controlled his frustration by remembering Ryan's words. *Under no circumstances will you use your true strength.*

They spent hours fighting until the dusty clock on the gym wall read seven in the evening. That's where Ryan called it for the night, standing perfectly comfortably with merely a small sweat stain on his shirt. Zenrot sat on the floor with his shirt drenched in sweat, trying to catch his breath. They hadn't talked during their fight, but Ryan offered his hand to help him stand one more time. Zenrot stood by himself, stalking out of the ring.

"Tomorrow, same routine." Ryan broke the silence. "You can eat what you please for today, if you'd like."

"Not hungry," he mumbled while heading to the exit door.

Ryan was surprised he wasn't hungry because he hadn't eaten all day. "Where are you going then?"

"Get a shower and sleep. I'm tired." He opened the door and was startled, nearly colliding with someone. Arashi was standing right in front of him. He bowed quickly. "Mr. Arashi! Forgive my rudeness. I was just finishing my training."

"Ah, that's good, my boy."

"Is there anything you need from me?"

"No! I was just passing by, you may carry on." Arashi stepped aside so he could pass.

"Thank you, sir." Zenrot took a step towards his bedroom but paused as the door swung closed behind him. His body was tired.

Arashi had been polite with Zenrot, but his expression changed when he faced Ryan. Even with the door closed, Zenrot could hear Arashi demanding an update on the status of their training. Ryan explained his methods; some Arashi agreed with, and others he did not. Through the door he could hear the general suggest that Zenrot should be trained according to the precise list Arashi had issued back in his office, but Ryan continued to disagree. While he explained how Zenrot had almost collapsed while they trained in the radioactive mist, Arashi cut Ryan off to acknowledge that he was worried, but seemed to write off the other man's concern, saying simply that this was his first try and he must be patient.

Zenrot couldn't keep listening to the conversation and continued the trek to his bedroom. He reached the building, quietly passed inside, and drifted down the empty hallway. When he reached his quarters door, he saw the plate number attached. "*04.*" It occurred to him that if he was staying in the fourth room, there must be other mutants staying in the building. He wondered who was in the rooms labeled "01" through "03." Ever since his arrival, he still hadn't seen any other mutants. His guess was that they were probably training with their majors. After all, Arashi had said each mutant had his own trainer suited to their combat style and, of course, their unique abilities.

He opened the door, walks inside his room, gently kicked the door shut, and stripped off his filthy training clothes. He tossed them into a hamper next to the bathroom door on his way to take a shower. Under the water, he took a couple of minutes to relax and think about tomorrow's training. Zenrot was pushing himself mentally, worried about the workouts Ryan expected for him to do. It felt almost impossible, even for a mutant.

Stepping out of the shower, while he was drying himself with a towel, someone knocked at the door. He wrapped the towel around his waist and trotted over, opening it. An old man, about seventy, was there. He was skinny, almost bald, and had a wrinkled face.

"I'm here to pick up the laundry," the old man said.

"Oh, sure. Let me get the hamper." He picks it up and handed it to the old man.

"I'll have it ready tomorrow at four in the morning. I'll leave it next to your door."

"Thank you very much, sir." Zenrot said as the old man walked to the next door. Just before he was about to close the door, Zenrot noticed the old man knocked on room "03"—and it opened. He peeked to see who it was but couldn't make out their face. The figure had long, straight black hair. Thin white arms handed a basket full of clothes to the old man and, on top of the basket, he could make out what appeared to be a bra almost slipping off the pile of clothes.

"Another mutant?" he said softly. As the old man departed, the unknown woman slipped back inside her room and forcefully shut the door. Zenrot closed his door in turn, deciding to ignore the situation and goes to sleep. He got dressed and tucked himself in bed just as someone once again knocked at his door. "Are you kidding me?" he snapped, setting the sheet aside and walking fast to the door. He quickly opened it, already interrogating whoever was on the other side. "Is it another service? Can it wait until—"

"Well… good to see you too."

"Bra—Brandolf?" He was surprised at the unexpected visit.

"May I come in?" The soldier grinned. "I brought snacks."

Zenrot waved as a sign to come inside but felt a flutter of nerves at seeing a non-mutant there. "Are you even supposed to be here?"

"Nope, but I sure am hungry, and thought you might be hungry too." Brandolf sat on the bed and pulled the food out of the bag. He offered, but Zenrot refused to eat. He glared, knowing Zenrot was hungry, then threw a sandwich at Zenrot.

He caught it in the air, his stomach growling at just the idea of eating. He couldn't resist the food. He unwrapped the sandwich and ate it like there was no tomorrow.

Once finished, he looked at Brandolf, "What brings you here?"

"Well, it's been months since the last time we saw each other. To be honest, this is probably the last time I'll have to check up on you for a while." He explained that Arashi would be sending troops to fight against Sentry Run soon. New mutants had been located in a different sector and Sentry Run was sending heavy troops to wipe them out. While the soldiers confronted this new force, Arashi was working on a strategy to attack Sentry Run's headquarters directly.

Zenrot saw an opportunity and asked if he could help in the battle, but Brandolf denied the request, saying that Zenrot must continue his training to become the mutant Arashi wanted.

He looked at the floor, worried, impatient, and afraid that it would take too long for Ryan to fully prepare him; that he would be unable to help those in need. Zenrot reminded him he defeated a Spartan right inside Art Gun's base and that should be enough. He insisted on sneaking out to lend them a hand.

Brandolf felt pleased that Zenrot really wanted to help, but even if he had defeated a Spartan, that wasn't enough compared to conditions in the field. He repeated that Zenrot must finish his training with Ryan.

Zenrot stood up from the side of his bed, frustrated, and explained what happened on his first day. He had failed at almost everything because it was all impossible in the first place. He was starting to believe that Ryan didn't know what he was doing, and that it might be for the best if he changed to another major.

Brandolf was silent, letting Zenrot to speak his mind freely. Brandolf could tell he'd been through a lot and listened and waited until Zenrot was out of words. "May I say something about it?" Brandolf said softly.

"Be my guest," he said, displeased.

"I've trained with Ryan, about two years ago. His training was very difficult for me since I was a skinny bastard back then." Zenrot chuckled, finding that hard to believe. "It's true, most of his training is quite a challenge. Others passed but me, to be honest, I thought I was never going to become a soldier. However, Ryan made his training harder. He was tough, rude, and mean... but he did it to get the best out of me." He stood up, walked to Zenrot, and laid his hand on his shoulder. "What I'm trying to say is that he knows how to push someone to release the best version of themselves. It may seem impossible, but he'll do whatever it takes to make it happen. Believe it or not, he wants the best for you."

Zenrot faced Brandolf. "How are you so sure of that?"

He whispered into Zenrot's ear, "Because he's the one who sent me here to make sure you ate." Zenrot gasped as Brandolf met his gaze and winked like a conspirator letting him in on the plan. He walked to the exit. "Plus, it really was a perfect chance for me to see you again. I wish you the best of luck!" he said, opening the door to leave.

"Wait!" Zenrot yelled. Brandolf stopped, leaning in the half-opened door. He looked back and noticed Zenrot was standing more confidently. He smiled and said, "I hope you make it back in one piece, so you can witness me as an official member of the MSF."

Brandolf smiled and nodded enthusiastically. "Sure thing!

Rest well, my friend." Brandolf left the room and closed the door.

"Friend…" Zenrot said to himself. For the first time, someone had called him a friend. It was nice for him to know he had someone he could trust—or at least have someone around that didn't despise him. He went to bed and quickly fell asleep, ready for the second day of training. If the first day had gotten off to a bad start, the second would be a chance to make a better effort.

CHAPTER SEVEN

The clock read 4:22 a.m. and Zenrot was getting ready. He picked up the uniform that the old man had left, cleaned, next to Zenrot's door. He needed to be at the gate of the Art Gun compound at 5:00 a.m. and still needed to make it there from the residence building. Zenrot would have to move with a purpose to get there on time.

He walked out of his room, locking the door behind him. As he turned toward the building exit, he noticed the door of room "03" was open. A woman walked out and pulled the door shut. She looked very young, almost Zenrot's age. Her hair was long, straight, and black, and was currently tied into a ponytail. She was dressed casually, and some bruises showed on her arms. Everything she wore was black: a black t-shirt with suspenders that held on to her black and gray cargo pants, and black boots. Zenrot saw a custom backpack that had five daggers, all of different sizes, attached. She looks to her right, noticing she was being watched. Zenrot didn't say a word and she just sniffed before heading out of the building.

Damn, she looked pissed. Zenrot looked at his watch—4:48 a.m. "Shit, I have to go to the gate fast!" He ran as fast as he could to get there in time. As he approached, he could see Ryan waiting at the gate in the distance. He came to a sliding stop in front of Ryan. "Am I late?" he asked desperately.

Ryan looked at his watch. "4:59 a.m."

Zenrot exhaled in relief.

"Overslept?" the major asked.

"No, sir! Encountered someone along the way."

"I see…" His watch started ringing. "Well, it's 5:00 a.m. Let's get going." He turned and walked the same path as he had yesterday.

Does he really have to be this cold? he thought as he followed the older man. They reached the same place as the day before and began training. Ryan sat on a rock, pulled his notebook from his backpack, and started taking notes of the results.

Zenrot started his first routine, climbing. He was moving faster and got a little higher than his first try but, unfortunately, fell again. Multiple times. Ryan signaled to keep trying and noted that Zenrot hadn't protested—he was maintaining his motivation, pumped to keep going until he reached his goal. After countless tries, Ryan signaled to stop and move on to the next event. The crumbling ground.

Zenrot was jumping and moving at maximum speed. He fell from the high ground and headed back to the start. "Permission to try one more time, sir?" he asked, staring straight at the road and ready to move.

"Permission granted," Ryan answered. Zenrot took off before the major was even done speaking. Ryan kept track, noting that he was moving faster. For the first time, Zenrot reached the end of the field but, when he was returning, slipped and fell. It was an improvement but, looking at the clock, he had still run out of time.

"That's enough for this section," he shouted from a distance. "Let's continue with a new exercise." Zenrot jumped his way back to Ryan. "Next, I want you to pick up the heaviest rock." There was one as big as a truck. Zenrot grabbed the rock with his hands and squeezed it with his fingers, careful not to squeeze too deep so it didn't bust to pieces. "I want you to start doing squats while holding that rock." Zenrot raised the rock up above his head and began doing squats.

"What's the limit, sir?" Zenrot asked, breathing hard from the exertion.

"Until I see your legs crumble and the rock squashes you. Go, go, GO!" he yelled to keep pressure on Zenrot and never took his eyes from the mutant. Twenty squats… fifty squats… one hundred squats. "I want you to do them slowly. I want you to feel those muscles. Come on, keep going!" His legs trembled, his hands shook, and every inhale and exhale was a momentous effort. "Come on, give me a few more—you can do it!" Ten squats… twenty-five squats… forty-seven extra squats. Zenrot's arms were about to fail. Sweat poured all over his face, his muscles hurt, and his veins were popping out. He couldn't hold on much longer. "Come on! Give me at least three more! THREE MORE!"

"I... I can't." He gasped, trying to catch his breath.

"Yes, you can! You can do it because I know you can! Come on! DO IT!" One... two... and, with all his strength, three. Zenrot threw the rock away and fell to the ground to catch his breath. "You did well. Five minutes of break." Ryan sounded proud, like the praise really came from his heart. Zenrot had achieved 150 squats with a giant rock on top of him, persevering despite an immense weight over his shoulders. He had really done it. Zenrot put a smile on as he breathed. "Remember you still need to lift the rock you left in the river."

Zenrot's smile faded away as he looked at Ryan. "With all due respect sir, you sure know how to be an ass, killing the mood like that."

Ryan laughed in genuine excitement. Surprisingly, he was having fun. "Well, Zenrot..." he said sarcastically as he walked toward him. "You better get used to it. Because we're going to be training together for a month until I get the best of you." He offered his hand to help him stand.

"Good." Zenrot smiled once again, grabbing the major's hand. "Because I'm ready for the challenge."

***

They had been training outside Art Gun's base for three weeks. Ryan continued pushing Zenrot to break his limits, and the results were measurably improved. He climbed the giant rocks the fastest way possible—almost as if Zenrot didn't need any ledges to grab with his hands. He learned to run lightweight at a speed of fifty miles per hour. If Zenrot trained hard enough and focused, Ryan was convinced he might be able to run up the walls.

The next observation was Zenrot's strength. He could carry most of the heaviest obstacles and routinely lifted them without struggle. To prove his strength, Ryan aimed with his right hand at a giant rock, ordering Zenrot to blow it up with a single punch. He took a firm position, slowly moving his right arm back with his fist, and cleanly punched the rock. It started cracking then, slowly, crumbled into pieces. Zenrot turned to look at Ryan; he looked impressed, but not convinced.

The two things remaining to complete all his training were to successfully survive in and navigate the radioactive mist for five minutes and to hold his breath underwater for ten minutes while lifting the giant rock. Aside those tasks, Zenrot was learning every fighting technique to improve his skills as well.

Zenrot questioned one of the trainings he still needed to accomplish. He understood the purpose of training in the radioactive mist, but Zenrot couldn't grasp why it was so important to lift a giant rock underwater. Ryan explained that the rock was to help him with his strength. Zenrot may have been able to carry heavy stuff easily in the open air, but underwater the object was twice as heavy. Additionally, staying underwater to hold his breath for a long period of time would help Zenrot escape from dangerous situations.

 Ryan checked on his notes and noticed they had about a week to finish. "Time is running out," he said out loud, looking sharply at Zenrot. Without hesitating, he said, "We still need to work on your survival skills during a CBRNE situation and your underwater training. Let's try to finish everything in less than the month so we can have more time left to experience real combat training. If we're successful, it'll leave us with a few days to rest."

"Yes, sir." Zenrot trained over and over for almost a week on surviving the CBRNE trial. Every time he felt something strange in his body, Zenrot focused on breathing the slowest way possible to adapt to the environment. He seemed dizzy but was still standing. Ryan wore a gas mask to keep an eye on how he was reacting and keep track of time. It had been much more than five minutes—eighteen minutes, exactly.

"You have done well," Ryan said proudly. "Let's get out of this place." He signaled with his hand to leave the area and walked out of the mist with Zenrot following.

"Don't you want to continue? We still have like an hour or two," Zenrot said, motivated.

"I admire your enthusiasm, but you have been under the mist for many attempts just today. You may have some side effects to work through and you need to recover. You will need your strength and focus."

"But I feel fine—"

"We're done, mister!" he shouted.

"*Geez*, sorry, major."

Both were clear of the mist. Finally in the fresh air, the sunset was clear and visible to both of them. Ryan removed his backpack, took off his gas mask, and returned it to its case inside the backpack. Then he stood up and held the bag in front of Zenrot. "But since you insist on keeping working, you'll carry this on our way back."

"Don't you mean doing your chores, sir?" Zenrot said, glaring at him with a smirk on his face.

Ryan pushed him lightly with the backpack and forced Zenrot to grab it. "Don't be absurd and let's go!" He went on ahead and Zenrot followed, the pair walking away from their training spot and heading between the trees to avoid detection. They didn't speak to each other all the way back to Art Gun. Zenrot was very anxious and wanted to ask him about his improvement but, at the same time, was afraid to ask since Ryan wasn't someone to look at the positive side on most occasions. Only time would tell. Zenrot remembered the girl he saw back at his residence. He hadn't seen her ever since, nor had he noticed any other mutants around.

"Major Ryan..." he said, finally breaking the silence between them. "Permission to ask a question, sir?"

"Didn't you ask a question just now?" he said sarcastically and with a chuckle. Zenrot gave him a stare, annoyed, yet wanted to laugh. "I'm just messing with you. What is it?"

"Are there any other mutants living in the building I'm staying in? I've only witnessed one mutant, couldn't see her face clearly though. I thought maybe there were more mutants around."

Ryan stayed silent for a minute and Zenrot was worried, thinking he had asked something he shouldn't have. "From what I've heard, there are four mutants assigned to the MSF, including you," Ryan answered, then added, "However, I haven't met the other mutants. Anyone who's not a mutant isn't allowed to go inside that building—unless it's an authorized worker or Arashi himself."

"I see…" He went from gazing down as he walked to raising his head and, with enthusiasm, saying, "Since you're training me… that means you are authorized to enter my quarters and find out who they are?"

"I'm afraid not." His voice changed to a low, almost-frightened tone. "Ever since the incident back in the warehouse, Arashi has been strict with mutant safety. I know a few soldiers back then weren't nice to you. Some soldiers weren't nice with other mutants as well. Arashi made it clear for the non-mutants not to mistreat anyone any longer. Besides that, it may be for the best."

"And why is that?" Zenrot said doubtfully.

"I'll be honest with you, Arashi wasn't pleased when you chose me as your trainer."

Zenrot was surprised. "But why?" he shouted. "I've learned so many things from you."

"Probably because I won't do a good job to get you prepared on time."

"Look…" Zenrot walked faster, passing some bushes to walk next to Ryan. "Even though sometimes you are mean as hell, I picked you because I know you will train me to be the best. Even if the other majors presented back then could do a tremendous job… I believed it was the best choice I've made so far. Arashi may not agree, but you are the only one on this whole base I can trust."

Zenrot could see Ryan smile slightly but didn't know if was because he was flattered or was taking it as a joke. Even if they had been together for a long period of time, Zenrot still couldn't guess what Major Ryan felt when he spoke his opinion.

"I can promise you this…" Ryan said, "I can't guarantee I'll make you the strongest mutant. But you have my word I'll do my best not only to make you a great mutant soldier of Art Gun… but also, a better person."

"I mean… I'm not a human, so…"

"Oh! You know what I mean!" Ryan shouted and Zenrot exploded into laughter, taking a few steps away to make sure he wasn't smacked in the head or something.

"I won't let you down." Zenrot spoke with certainty, gazing at Ryan with a smirk on his face. "So, this means you'll be less mean?"

"Don't push it! You still need discipline so you can improve more than what you already have."

"So that means I've—"

"We're here." Ryan interrupted, noticing that they'd arrived at Art Gun. "I'll be heading on my way to work on tomorrow's schedule. Remember to eat and get some sleep. I need you well rested for your last underwater training. After we achieve our goal, I need to search for your new uniform and analyze what weapons and gadgets you will need for your final combat training." As he finished talking, he departed, leaving Zenrot behind.

Zenrot's doubts had left. Ryan somehow had admitted Zenrot had gotten better with time. Not through the exact words Zenrot had expected but, coming from Ryan, that was enough. *"I must get better tomorrow. I have to…"*

***

The next day, Zenrot and Ryan were at the lake. Ryan sat on a rock nearby while Zenrot was in the deep part of the lake trying to lift the giant rock. He was ignoring the fact that he needed to hold his breath while lifting, focusing all his strength on pulling the rope up with both hands. He pulled, floating, with all his strength. Finally, in an almost perceptible shift, he felt the rock lift from the ground. Holding the rope tight, Zenrot kept pulling as he swam upward using only his legs. Tightness in his chest reminded him he needed to breathe. Zenrot looked up and could barely see the light of the sun. It was a long way to go, but he wasn't going to give up.

Come on you stupid rock, lift! Zenrot held the rope with one hand and swam with the other up to go faster. His arm started to hurt so he switched to grab the rope with both hands. Stalled and floating, the rock began to fall slowly back down. *Hell no!* Zenrot gripped the rope tighter and pulled himself up.

On the surface, Ryan was waiting for Zenrot to show up. He was looking at his watch and noticed he'd been a long time underwater. "Come on Zenrot, you can do this…"

Zenrot was slowly swimming higher and could clearly see the light of the sun. *I'm almost there!* His lungs hurt and he was about to faint. Zenrot was passing tired and approaching exhaustion. A cramp in his left arm hurt his grip, and the rope slipped from his hand. *NO!* He twisted and dove down, grabbing the rope and tying it onto his waist. He swam. Even swimming as fast as he could, though, Zenrot started to slow down. Dizziness was overtaking him. He accidently opened his mouth, swallowing a lot of water.

The faint light at the surface faded as he fainted. The rock, tied to his waist, dragged him all the way back to the bottom of the lake.

In the gloom, a voice both unfamiliar and strangely comforting sounded deep in Zenrot's unconscious mind.

"Zenrot...... Rise...... It is not the time...... Not yet...... Rise...... Rise......RISE!"

Zenrot woke up, closed his mouth, and untied the rope. His hands were glowing with a dark violet aura, and his red eyes shone even brighter. Bubbles burst out of Zenrot's nose and hands from the intensity of his aura. The veins of his arms showed clearly while he held the rope, gritting his teeth as he pulled the hardest he could. His aura grew brighter and brighter as a single thought repeated like a mantra through Zenrot's mind.

To hell with this rock! Zenrot pulled with his maximum strength and *threw*.

Ryan was looking down at the river, worried for Zenrot. He saw something rising from the depths, getting closer and closer. Realizing it was the giant rock, he dashed from the shore, watching in awe as the boulder passed high into the sky before arcing gracefully to the beach and fell next to him. When it hit the ground, dust flew everywhere, and Ryan started coughing. It was hard to see, but he kept his gaze on the water. Zenrot came out and rested at the edge of the lake. "Zenrot!" Ryan ran as fast he could and pulled him out of the water. Zenrot was coughing and trying hard to breathe. "Are you all right?" Ryan asked, noticing the glow surrounding the mutant's hands.

"Did I reach the goal?" Zenrot asked softly.

"Yes, you broke the goal... twelve minutes underwater." He looked back over his shoulder. "And you took the rock out of the lake."

Zenrot coughed. "I must say... fuck yeah..." He slowly stood, and Ryan took care to help him regain his balance. Zenrot stalked toward the giant rock he had thrown, looks at it closely, then punched it hard enough to shatter the boulder into small pieces. No trace of it was left. "Never again." He looked at Ryan over his shoulder, then turned fully around. When Ryan saw the expression in his red eyes, he realized his student had become another person. Someone who was more motivated and wasn't afraid of anything. He was ready.

"So, what's our next move?" Zenrot asked.

Ryan gave a sharp smirk. "Now, we get you ready for battle."

CHAPTER EIGHT

After their last training, Zenrot and Ryan arrived back at base. When they reached the entrance, one of Arashi's bodyguards was waiting for their arrival. Ryan noticed his presence and told Zenrot to stay behind while he went to speak with the bodyguard. It was a short conversation; it appeared that the bodyguard said what he had to say and left. Ryan walked back to Zenrot.

"Looks like Arashi wants to discuss some things," Ryan said. "You should head back to your residence and get some rest. I'll meet you outside at eight in the morning and give you the details about our next step."

Zenrot noticed he was acting strange, picking up on a note of what sounded like fear in his voice. "Is there something wrong?" Zenrot asked. "You sure you don't want me to go with you?"

"That's above your paygrade." Zenrot gave a blank stare to Ryan. "Don't worry, I'll be fine. Get some rest, that's an order," he said flatly. Zenrot saluted by standing straight, snapping his right hand sharply to a position beside his right eye. Ryan nodded and took off in a sprint on his way to Arashi's office. Zenrot realized that the major had left his belongings.

"Sir! Your backpack—"

"Take it with you! I'll pick it up tomorrow!" Ryan shouted in return.

Zenrot had no choice but to take it with him. He walked to his room and, as usual, entered the empty hallway—empty except for the cleaner's equipment. He was probably cleaning a room, making everything as spotless as Zenrot usually found it.

Zenrot walked to his room, searching his pockets for the key. A reckless noise came from the main door. He gasped and turned right to see what it was; the girl from the next room was walking towards her door. She had scratches on her arms, blood all over her uniform, and some small bruises on her face. She looked like she was coming from a devastating fight, but was walking like nothing happened. The cleaner came out from the room labeled "02."

"Ma'am…" the cleaner said, approaching. "Are you in need of assistance?"

"No." she said flatly, facing her door. "Make sure to pick up my clothes and have them ready for tomorrow."

"Why, of course, ma'am," the cleaner said politely.

She opened the door, went inside, and slammed it so hard you could hear the echo. *Damn she was rude.* The cleaner noticed Zenrot's presence and asked if he needed anything or if he could assist him. Zenrot said there was no need, only that he was looking for his key. The cleaner approached his door and opened it with his spare. Zenrot nodded in appreciation of his assistance, searched through his pocket again, finding a snack bar. He handed it to the cleaner.

"Here," he said while giving the snack.

"Oh, don't worry, sir, I'm just doing my job."

"Nonsense, I was irresponsible for losing my keys, so please take it as a token of my gratitude. It's not much but I'd like to show I appreciate the help." He rolled his eyes, glancing at the door next to his. "Plus, also for trying to help that rude woman."

The cleaner snorted and quickly covered his mouth to avoid being disrespectful. He gratefully accepted Zenrot's offer, grabbing the snack bar and bowing in thanks. He rose, looking at Zenrot curiously. The cleaner said, "You aren't like the other mutants I've met around here. You have a good heart."

"Nah, I'm just showing respect to those who work hard for us mutants, and for the sake of others." Then he snapped, realizing what the cleaner said. *The other mutants I've met.* Now he could sate his curiosity. "Say..." Zenrot said, drawing out the word. "If you don't mind me asking, how many mutants are in this building?"

His mood changed at Zenrot's question. "I'm not supposed to give *any* information while working at this building," the cleaner answered.

"I see..." Zenrot said, disappointed and with his head lowered.

The cleaner looked side to side, making sure there was no one else. He walked on his way to room "01" and knocked a couple times. "Room service." He waited for a few seconds, but no one answered. So far, he believed the girl wouldn't come out of her room after having seen her condition. The cleaner walked back to Zenrot and whispered, "If I say something, you must promise me you won't tell anyone." Zenrot nodded, affirming he'd keep the promise. "There are four mutants in total, including you. One is the girl you just saw, and the other two are males. Barely seen in this place."

"Why is that?"

"I don't know. Probably has to do with their training. Sometimes I've seen them in here perfectly fine, and sometimes brutally hurt—or even worse."

"No medical attention? They're just left like that?" Zenrot asked, irritated but also worried about their safety.

"There is medical assistance… but I know they don't feel safe. Remember, not many humans agree about working alongside mutants. Even if the people around here are claiming to help the mutant race, there are still bad people. I know *her*—" The cleaner stared at the girl's door, then looked back at Zenrot. "—for example, she hates any medical treatment from the base. There were times the soldiers had to force her, and some ended up injured."

"I see…"

"I can't blame her." He obviously felt bad for the girl, but after a moment snapped back to the present and remembered his duty. "I better get back to work. My advice, young lad… be careful who you choose to trust." He grabbed his cart of supplies. "We're at war right now. Someone may be an ally for today, but on the next day? They could be your enemy. Best of luck, mate."

The cleaner walked away, pushing the cart.

"Today a friend, tomorrow an enemy..." he whispered to himself. Zenrot walked to his room and locked the door. After a shower he got ready to sleep. He lay on his bed with his arm crossed behind his head, thinking about how the world would be if mutants and humans got along. Sadly, Zenrot didn't know what it would be like. Deep down he was glad to fight alongside someone who wanted to protect those who were different, but what was the point to fight along humans who were *forced* to help the mutants? If only it came from their heart.

Zenrot smiled faintly and closed his eyes. *One way or another... I will make a difference for the mutants and make the world get along. That's a promise.*

***

Two hours before Zenrot had arrived at his residence, Ryan stepped into the elevator with a bodyguard to meet Arashi. They reached the last floor and, when the doors opened, the bodyguard signaled to move forward. As Ryan got close, Arashi looked sharply at Ryan. The general was sitting on his desk with his hands together, steepled in front of his mouth. Normally, Arashi was working on something when someone approached directly. This wasn't a good sign.

Ryan and the bodyguard reached the front of the desk. "Thank you, you may depart," Arashi said to the bodyguard. The man nodded and retreated to his usual position. Arashi looked straight at Ryan as he placed his hands on his desk. "How is our boy Zenrot?"

Ryan bowed to him. "He's doing really well, sir. His results are improving greatly. Tomorrow he will be getting fitted for his gear and training for realistic combat. Once that's done, he'll be ready for battle."

"Have any other special abilities been discovered during training?"

"Running very fast, sir."

"How fast?"

"Fifty-five miles per hour, sir."

Arashi hummed very low, then said, "Not *that* fast. One of the other MSF has run seventy-five miles per hour. But it'll do."

"Also…" Ryan continued speaking, "some strange, dark violet aura came from his hands. Kind of like he was releasing energy to increase his strength. It seems like Zenrot can't take full control of it." When Ryan gave that detail, it sparked something in Arashi's mind. He stood, hitting the desk with his hands.

"I knew it!" His tone was enthusiastic as he walked away from his desk, desperately pacing from one side to the other. "Somehow, I had a feeling he possessed more than just massive strength. We know he has a decent speed enhanced run. Now we know he releases an aura energy—only it hasn't truly developed. Maybe his memory loss has something to do with it. Hmm… a dark aura…" Arashi stopped walking and turns directly to Ryan. "How did he release it? Was it like shooting from his hands?"

"No. I only saw them glow when he came out of the water throwing the giant rock."

Arashi faced the ground, thoughtful, "That means he's having trouble releasing the energy from his body…" He looked up again at Ryan. "Maybe it's best if you leave the rest of his training with—"

"With all due respect, sir..." Ryan interrupted, making sure Arashi didn't finish that sentence. "I still have a week left to train him properly. He has to learn to battle with—and without—his special abilities."

Arashi's expression changed. He raised his eyebrows and looked at Ryan with derision. "Remember your place, major. I need *him* with *all* his abilities."

"My apologies, General Arashi, but I think it is best if we stick to the program. Even if there's more in Zenrot, rushing his training won't make any difference. The abilities presented have been showing up during his training program outside of Art Gun. If you insist on finding a way to make him release the dark aura from his hands," Ryan spoke with attitude, but in a deliberately pacifying tone. He had an idea. "Maybe if we create something to help Zenrot release his energy; something that can make him focus without exhausting or draining his reserves. It might help him learn to control how much energy he can use." It was objectively a good suggestion to help Zenrot manage his abilities.

Arashi calmed down yet was still unhappy about how Ryan spoke to him. He walked to sit back on his desk calmly, placing his hands together. "And how do you suggest we help him control his abilities?"

"Well, he's trained for close combat… All that's left is ranged combat." He snapped his fingers, indicating he had the perfect idea. "How about a gun specialized for Zenrot? Using his aura to shoot and reload instead of using bullets and a magazine. That will help Zenrot to control his energy and not overdo himself. If he practices hard enough, Zenrot can become even stronger and wipe out Sentry Run's heavy resistance with a single blast!" Ryan thought it was a great idea, but Arashi's expression looked like he was still not convinced. He leaned back in his chair and stared at Ryan for a full minute in complete silence. Ryan felt nothing but fear.

"If you knew about inventions and not just training recruits, you probably would've been on my science team," Arashi finally said, breaking the silence. "What's the schedule for you and Zenrot?"

"Tomorrow at 8:00 a.m. with the Blacksmith. I'll get him what he needs to be ready."

Arashi took a moment to consider. "Very well," he decreed. "I will confer with the head scientist and suggest your idea for our boy. Make sure he's ready. You are dismissed." Ryan bowed and walked smartly to the elevator.

Once he was far enough away from the desk, Arashi called his bodyguards back to the office via the radio. Arashi kept observing Ryan, making sure he left through the elevator. Laying back in his chair, he rubbed his goatee and waited.

A few minutes later, the elevator arrived. When it opened, Mojo, along with the returning bodyguards, arrived. Mojo sprinted his way to Arashi while the bodyguards walked at a more reasonable pace.

"Ryan said you need me for an invention," Mojo said with a mix of anxiety and excitement. Arashi explained what Ryan had suggested about the gun and that Mojo must invent something for Zenrot. Mojo was pleased; it was a chance to invent for someone he was excited to work with. When Arashi told him he had until eight in the morning, Mojo was shocked at how little time he had. His watch read 11:30 p.m. which only gave him a few hours to finish the special weapon. Mojo begged for more time and a chance to study the boy, but Arashi didn't budge. He also reminded the scientist that he wasn't allowed to go near Zenrot. "But Arashi, how am I supposed to work on something for the boy if I don't know what he's capable of?"

"You'll figure something out. You did it with the last two mutants."

"But that was completely different. Zenrot is a special kind of mutant, I can feel it."

"And that's why I want you to stay away from him," Arashi said, signaling one of his bodyguards closer. He whispered into his ear and the bodyguard nodded before walking away. "I don't want any more of your dirty work. Is that clear?"

Mojo lowered his head, not making eye contact. "Yes, sir." He walked, departing for the lab. Just as he was about to reach the elevator, Arashi shouted, reminding him the weapon must be done for tomorrow, and that he had great expectations for Zenrot. When Mojo stepped inside the elevator, he turned to face the closing doors. In the distance, Arashi's face had changed. No words were needed; the look was a clear threat indicating that the gun had better work or there would be consequences. The elevator doors closed, and Mojo finally left.

Arashi took a deep breath, lay back on the chair with his legs crossed on top of the desk, and began drumming on it with the fingers of one hand. Gazing down at his MSF folders, a paper was sticking out, displaying a name and date.

Last name: UNKNOWN, First name: ZENROT.
Date of birth: UNKNOWN, Date found: APRIL 21, 1965.

Arashi raised an eyebrow, smirked, and chuckled softly. He turned around in his chair and looked through the window. *"I can't wait to see how this will change everything. Soon, I'll have the perfect army."*

CHAPTER NINE

With five minutes left until eight o'clock in the morning, Zenrot grabbed Ryan's backpack and walked to the door. He was dressed in his uniform, only one step away from becoming an official MSF member who represented an example of a good mutant. He was a bit excited, yet more nervous than ever. Zenrot didn't like the idea of taking lives, even if he had only destroyed robots so far. He didn't want to see people killing each other either, though, and was desperate to be able to make a difference. He trotted through the hallway on the way to the entrance and, stepping outside, saw Ryan was already waiting in front of the residence. He was always sharp with time.

"Ready to go?" Ryan asked and Zenrot nodded, handing the backpack to Ryan and following. Ryan handed a small wrapped package to Zenrot, telling him he would no longer wear the regular uniform. Starting today, he was to use the MSF uniform. Zenrot immediately wanted to open the package to see how it looked. It wasn't something to be excited about, considering they were at war, but he was gladdened the hard work had actually paid off.

Ryan also mentioned Zenrot needed to pick a last name. He was confused by that at first, but Ryan explained since he was an official member of the MSF, Arashi would want to fill the paperwork in with a full name so that, when the time came, people could remember who the mutants that fought for greatness were. At first, it sounded to Zenrot like he was going to die once he was outside, but then he thought it through carefully. Ryan was describing keeping history records of the war. Zenrot had never thought about having a last name, though. If there was one in his past, he couldn't remember it. Seeing his distress at having trouble remembering if he had a surname, Ryan suggested picking one for himself since there was no record whatsoever. Zenrot thought it was a great idea, but after a few minutes of thinking, he had no candidates. He asked Ryan if he had any suggestions, but the major didn't want to recommend any last names Zenrot might think were "horrible". Zenrot insisted, knowing that Ryan wouldn't make the mistake of choosing a bad name.

"Are you sure about this?" Ryan asked.

"Of course," Zenrot said, hyped. "Besides, I know for a fact that you can choose one better than me."

"If that's the case... you may be right about that."

"Hey!" He turned towards Ryan and narrowed his eyes into a glare.

Ryan laughed heartily until he calmed down. "I mean, you're the one who said it, not me." He took a minute to think for a good last name, something that would suit and describe him.

Finally, he had an idea. "How about Bellator?"

Zenrot raised an eyebrow, surprised by the choice. "Bellator? What does that mean?"

"It means *'warrior'* in Latin. First, I thought of *miles* which means 'soldier,' but it's too literal and it sounds like a second name."

He laughed softly. "Zenrot Bellator... I like how it sounds."

Ryan gave a short smile as they came to a stop. "Well, I'm glad you like it." He tilted his head forward so Zenrot would look. "We're here."

They were in front of the local gun shop. The windows were heavily tinted, and something about the store made Zenrot a little nervous. His hands floated next to his hip, and he found himself moving his fingers around to calm himself. He looked at Ryan, asking why the gun shop had tinted glass if everyone knew it has weapons. Ryan explained that the blacksmith didn't like to be watched, nor did he like anyone to stare into his store.

Ryan pulled the door open and walked inside. Zenrot followed, asking himself *why Ryan kept calling the owner a blacksmith if he only worked with guns. Shouldn't it be gunsmith?* When he got inside, he was in shock. Zenrot stood in amazement with his mouth opened wide as he browsed the store. At his right there was a wall full of guns: Colt M16, Colt XM148, Stoner 63, and many other choices. On his left were all the knives, daggers, swords, and any other melee weapon he could imagine. At the front of the store there was a counter that separated the room. Behind the counter there was a door, and it looked like there's more to it, though it was marked for authorized personnel only.

The walls were covered in uniforms and variations of armor, from lightweight to heavy resistance.

Ryan went to the counter and knocked on top of it. "Grim!" He kept knocking, calling out the name many times. "GRIM!"

"I'm coming, damn it!" someone yelled from behind the door. Footsteps moved closer, then *BAM!* Someone busted the door open. It was a man about forty, in a military uniform, though surprisingly not presentable. His clothes were filled with stains and looked not to have been cleaned in days. He was a little chubby, had black and white hair, a scrappy beard, and big hands. One of those large hands was wrapped around a screwdriver; apparently, he had been working on something. Zenrot noted bags under his eyes, like he hadn't slept in days. "You always come at the worst time, major!" His yelled response was angry.

"Good to see you too, Grim," Ryan said very seriously and went straight to the point. He looked over his shoulder at Zenrot, patted him on the back, and pushed him close to the counter. "Grim, this is Zenrot Bellator. Zenrot, this is Grim."

Zenrot nodded a greeting.

"Ah, the new mutant." Grim was not impressed by his appearance. He scanned him up and down, a funny look on his face.

"Then you know why we're here," Ryan said firmly. Without any other words, Grim lifted a small portion of the counter so they could pass. They followed Grim to a very small room that had a horrible stench. Inside there were many tools and gadgets, but they were unfamiliar and weird looking to Zenrot.

There were weapons and accessories of a sort that weren't at the entrance and so many things laying on the floor that it was difficult to walk through. Grim went to a wide wooden table, sat on a chair, and continued working on what he had been adjusting with the screwdriver.

"I'll be with you in a few minutes; crazy scientist man handed me the blueprints of this gun at three in the morning, and the process was a pain in the ass," Grim said, struggling. While he worked on the gun, Ryan searched around for a tape measure. He found one on top of a cabinet and told Zenrot to stand straight, with his hand in the air to measure his body. His arms, chest, legs, and shoulders followed.

Zenrot was confused as to why Ryan was measuring almost every part of his body. "What's this for?"

"It's for your armor. You aren't fighting in just your uniform." Ryan stepped behind him and measured with the tape at about five feet and in a forty-five-degree angle. "All set. While we train, Grim will work on the rest of the equipment you need." He checked on Grim's work. "How much left?"

"Right about… now." Grim stood, pushing his chair away and walking towards Zenrot. "Here." He handed him the gun. Zenrot took it and examined the weapon.

Ryan didn't seem impressed, so much as actually disappointed at the results. "That's the greatest gun ever that you've been working on all night?" he said sarcastically, taking the gun from Zenrot's hands. "It looks like a regular gun to me… only… bigger?"

Grim smirked, grabbing the gun from Ryan's hands and giving it back to Zenrot. "The gun is designed to shoot bullets almost half an inch in size—zero point four-two-nine inches to be precise—or ten point nine millimeters if you're that finicky about knowing the size." Grim's tone was unpleasant, but he seemed familiar with Ryan's insistence on every detail. "The barrel is fifteen inches long and the handle should be comfortable for you to hold it well. You'll notice that the cylinder is a little bigger than usual, but it can handle the bullets just fine."

Although Ryan didn't notice much of a difference, Zenrot could feel that the customization was unique. There was something especially interesting about the grip panel and on the side of the handle. There was stainless steel and glass on the handle. It looked like it could break easily, but he was certain it was bulletproof. "What's the glass for?" Zenrot asked curiously.

"I'm glad you asked," Grim said, flattered. "When you release energy from your hands it absorbs the energy as ammunition. We didn't know how much energy you'd be able to release, so we had to improvise. If you keep your focus, you can choose the size of the energy bullets by concentrating your aura until the cylinder is full. The barrel will expand and sustain the energy for you to take the shot. The more energy you use, the bigger the shot."

"What happens if I hold it for too long? Wouldn't the gun explode?" Zenrot asked, the nervousness evident in his voice.

"That's one of the things Mojo and I worked all night on. When we finished production, he charged the gun with energy samples in his lab. This thing can hold enough to shoot a nuke. So…" He glares at Zenrot with a sharp smile. "I say it will hold enough. If you can surpass *that,* we can work on some upgrades later. For now, this will suffice. The only thing you need to remember is not to reload with ordinary bullets *and* use your energy. I assure you, it will blow up. You don't want to see charged explosives coming through the cylinder. I called it... the Energy Assimilator."

Zenrot looked at the gun in silence until Ryan decided to speak. "Why make a gun that uses regular bullets if they can't resist his energy? Why not make it *only* for his energy?" Ryan shouted at Grim, obviously worried for Zenrot's safety.

"Hey! Don't yell at me, major. We thought it was a good idea in case the boy can't use his energy. He still has a way to protect himself."

"Fair enough..." Ryan cooled his temper but was still worried. He asked if there could be any changes to the gun to increase safety.

Zenrot looked at Ryan and Grim. "Hey, major," he said calmly, interrupting their conversation. "It's all right. I think it's perfect." They were both surprised with his answer. He looked Grim straight in the eyes and nodded in gratitude. "Thank you for all the hard work, Grim. I'll use it very well." His tone was cheerful.

Grim sniffed in relief and visibly relaxed. "Thank you! At least someone appreciates my work," he said with a playful glare at Ryan and Zenrot while holding back a laugh.

Zenrot took a quick look at the uniform he was holding. The shirt was black with two vertical red stripes on his right. On the left side of the chest was a small Art Gun symbol, and the bottoms were a pair of black cargo pants. Looking back at his gun, Zenrot noticed the colors were silver and brown—like any other regular gun. He asked Grim if there was enough time to change the colors for the gun to match his uniform, and Grim told him he could change the design in a minute.

Zenrot bowed again in gratitude. "Thank you, Grim the Blacksmith," he said as politely as he could while handing over the gun. "Is there a place where I can change clothes?"

Grim felt very flattered for a minute and preened for a moment until Zenrot asked where to change. He pointed to a door hidden in the shadows where the bathroom was.

As Zenrot changed, Grim went to his fridge, grabbed a bottle of spray colors from on top of it, and sat back at his worktable to start painting. "You have a good kid, lad. I can see why you worry too much about him," he said to Ryan as he painted.

"I don't know what you're talking about, this is just a business matter," the major replied, bluntly.

Grim stopped to look over his shoulder at Ryan with an eyebrow raised. "Uh-huh. I ain't buying that bullshit." He continued painting. "Well, I am in no position to tell you what *business* you have with each other, but I must remind you not to get emotionally attached. You know Arashi has immense plans for the boy. Once he's ready, you won't see him anymore." Ryan went silent and lowered his head with sorrow. "I know he reminds you of your—"

"Don't you dare finish that sentence and get back to work!" Ryan snapped furiously. "Tell Zenrot I'll be waiting outside." He walked out of the shop.

"Damn, I never imagined triggering him that way".

***

Twenty minutes passed, enough time for Zenrot and Ryan to make it to the shooting range while Grim worked on Zenrot's body armor. Zenrot was wearing the new black and red uniform while practicing aiming with a Colt M16 rifle. In front of him there was a table with ammunition and a second gun; this one a Smith & Wesson model. Ryan was a few feet away, watching Zenrot shooting for target practice. Zenrot didn't struggle with aiming; all his targets were a handful of yards away. He repeatedly was able to alternate shooting them in the head and the heart with great speed and precision.

"Switch!" Ryan shouted.

Zenrot quickly put the rifle on the table, switching to the revolver. Only having six bullets, he knew he had to make sure each one counted for a target. Holding the weapon with both hands to keep the gun steady, he shot one bullet into the head of each target in front of him. As soon as he was out of bullets, he quickly reloaded by releasing the cylinder and shaking the old shells out of the magnum. He swept six bullets from the table with one hand and pressed them into the gun in one try. This time, he aimed the gun with only one hand and cycled his shots across the targets again. Not a single miss.

"Hold!" Ryan shouted. Zenrot lowered the gun. Ryan raised a hand and signaled the soldiers in the area to replace the targets with new ones. "Your aim is very impressive. Great speed and reflexes."

"Does this mean I can try my gun now?" he asked politely, laying on the charm.

"No," Ryan said flatly. He tightened his grip on the Energy Assimilator, reinforcing that Zenrot couldn't use it yet.

"Ah come on! They made the gun for a reason, and now it matches my uniform. At least just once!" The Energy Assimilator was now as black as charcoal, with the trigger, handle, a red line on the cylinder, and small red rings around the end of the barrel all a bold, matching red. Zenrot put the magnum on the table, turned to face Ryan and said, "I mean… am I even going to use these guns in battle? I thought mutants carried their unique weapons."

"They do. But if you're fighting against enemy soldiers and can't use your abilities, you must learn to use your enemy's weapons to your advantage. They may not be like ours, but most of them are similar. When you master your shooting skills with most weapons, then I'll hand you the Energy Assimilator." As they spoke, the soldiers placed the targets 500 meters away. Ryan signaled to move them further away. 1,000 meters… Ryan continued waving. 1,500 meters.

He's joking, right? Zenrot thought with an eyebrow raised.

Ryan waved again. 2,000 meters.

Zenrot opens his eyes in surprise and looked at the major. "Don't you think that's a little too far?"

"Mm… You're right that the distance is off." He waved once and the targets were reset at 2,500 meters. "Now *that* is far enough."

Zenrot's jaw dropped at how far the targets were and got

desperate. "You've got to be kidding me, right?"

"Nope. I want to see how good your shooting is when the enemy is at a very long distance." He turned around and walked to a wooden box on the ground, then took the lid off. He placed the Energy Assimilator aside and pulled a sniper rifle out of the box, a Remington Model 700. He demonstrated to Zenrot how it worked and how to hold the rifle properly while laying down for stability and to minimize his own exposure. "I want you to hit the target in the head. You have two tries, then we change the exercise."

Zenrot took the sniper rifle and moved to the side of the table for a better position. He laid on the ground facing the distant target and held the sniper steady.

"Take your time and focus. Remember to breathe slowly," Ryan said calmly. Zenrot looked through the scope, his finger resting gently on the trigger. His target was in the sights. Ready, aim, and... *BAM.* Zenrot took the shot.

He steadied the weapon and looked through the scope again, searching for where the shot landed. On the right side of the chest. He had missed. Ryan, looking through binoculars, calmly directed, "Again." Zenrot aimed one more time, held his breath, and exhaled. He waited for a couple of seconds and... *BAM!*

Ryan looked through his binoculars, then lowered them down. "Not bad... You hit the mark, but you won't be using the sniper rifle anytime soon."

Zenrot glared at him. "Then why the hell are you training me with a sniper?"

"This wasn't a full sniper training—trust me. This was a test.

One of the MSF members can snipe five times faster than that—and hits their target without missing a shot. Arashi sent me a list of tests and results for you to work towards, but some of them depend on your skills, resistances, and abilities. The sniper training was to see how good your aim is… It's all right."

"You don't sound very convinced."

"With a sniper rifle, no." Ryan grabbed the Energy Assimilator from the box and stretched his arm to Zenrot. "Let's see if you're better with your gun."

Zenrot raised his eyebrows. "Are your certain, major?"

"Take it. Now is the time for you to test your energy limits." Zenrot grabbed the gun as his mentor cautioned, "Remember, you must not overuse your energy."

"How do I know where that point is?" Zenrot asked.

"Unfortunately, that's up to you. Remember, all mutants have energy inside, but it's not the same for everyone. It's like a different element or a different species. You saw aura coming from your hands… That's your strength. I don't know if you even noticed, but you used your energy to take that giant rock out of the lake. Maybe you'll discover more abilities you haven't figured out yet. But you must be careful not to overdo it. Sometimes, you may feel exhausted. Sometimes you can even faint. Or worse, sometimes it can kill you." Zenrot swallowed in fear. "I can show you how to be the best soldier, but learning to control your abilities is something you'll have to do yourself."

Zenrot noticed the change in Ryan's voice. He was talking softly and didn't sound like the major that had been pushing him to the edge. He looked worried for Zenrot's safety. He had only known about the aura coming from his hands for a few days, but Zenrot had told Ryan he would practice hard to control his energy. But he knows words aren't enough, too—Ryan always wanted results.

Zenrot turned, facing his target, and lifted the Energy Assimilator with both hands. Leveling it down range, he confidently asked, "Permission to take the first shot, Major Ryan?" His stance remained steady.

Ryan nodded and smirked. "Permission granted. Remember, focus your energy through the handle, let it flow to the cylinder, and when it is ready… take the shot." Zenrot focused, trying to remember what triggered him to release his aura. He thought about the struggle he went through back at the lake, how he almost lost himself deep in the water, and how he was not willing to quit. Slowly, a dark colored, glowing energy emerged from his hands.

Zenrot smiled. He was confident he could now control his energy.

"Good," Ryan said, "now try to transfer your energy to your gun." The energy flowed easily through the glass in the handle. Zenrot could feel the energy reshaping as its travelled inside the cylinder. Zenrot was about to pull the trigger. He could sense the barrel expanding. He took a deep breath and… *BAM!*

An energy bullet screamed its way toward the target. The soldiers nearby saw the bullet coming and scattered. When it struck the target, it exploded, blowing the whole thing away. Zenrot saw how it blew up and jumped in excitement. Ryan didn't have to use his binoculars; he saw the whole thing from where he was despite the distance. He laughed nervously. "Well... now, that's very impressive."

"You know what's funny?" Zenrot rubbed the back of his head with his hand, smiling with his eyes closed. "I don't even feel like I used much energy."

Ryan gave him a dead stare. "Well, now we will train until you're all drained for being cocky."

"I expected you to say something like that."

They both started laughing.

CHAPTER TEN

October 16, 1966

Zenrot only had two days left to complete his training. He was spending his time training with the Energy Assimilator and drilling combat training on the battlefield. His results had exponentially improved since his first day. Zenrot was fighting against ten well-trained soldiers in hand-to-hand combat and was not allowed to use weapons or his abilities. Ryan watched the fight from one side while Arashi observed from the other.

Two soldiers rushed towards Zenrot, throwing many punches at the same time. Zenrot blocked their attacks with his arms and, when he had an opening, dashed between the soldiers. He pivoted and grabbed both of their heads, smacking them together hard enough to knock both down. Another soldier had a long staff and swung at Zenrot from behind. Zenrot turned around, grabbing the stick with his left hand and pulling it toward him. He forced the soldier to come forward and kicked him square in the chest with his right foot. The soldier fell, and Zenrot punched him across the cheek to knock him out.

"Remember, do not use your full strength!" Ryan shouted from afar. "Defensive position!"

"Yes, sir!" Zenrot continued walking towards his opponents with the staff in his hands. He used it as a light weapon to prevent them from throwing punches. Five of his opponents moved close enough to engage, attacking from every direction. Zenrot retreated, dodging their attacks while taking opportunities to counter his enemies with strikes from the stick. Each opponent was hit a few times in different spots until none of them could stand—the whirling staff was effective in forcing them to lay low. They were all left on the ground moaning in pain as Zenrot took a defensive position waiting for the last two opponents. After a strategic moment, they surrendered and retreated. Zenrot threw the stick away and crouched to rest.

Ryan entered the fighting area, walking toward Zenrot and offering him a hand. He accepted and stood back up. "Well done, my boy," Ryan said, patting Zenrot's back. "You're officially ready."

The younger man took a deep breath and exhaled. Zenrot smiled, turning his head to look at Ryan. "Couldn't do it without a good teacher."

Before they could continue talking, they heard the sound of applause. The noise was getting closer and closer. "You fought extraordinarily. It looks like all the training has paid off," Arashi said, visibly satisfied with the results.

"Thank you, General Arashi, but this wouldn't have been

possible without Major Ryan," Zenrot said sincerely, giving all the credit to Ryan.

"Well, you're all set. Grim must've finished with your armor. So, let's get it and suit up. Tomorrow you officially start with the MSF crew." Arashi turned around, folding his hands behind his back and started to leave.

"Wait, tomorrow?" Ryan snapped and shouted, "General Arashi!"

The general stopped and looked over his shoulder.

"He has two days left of training—"

"He's ready, major. I've seen enough."

"I understand, but I think tomorrow he should take a break to rest."

"Rest?" Arashi turned fully around, facing Ryan and Zenrot with a strict expression. "We're at war, major. You think there is time for a break?" He raised his voice angrily and the soldiers who happened to be nearby took the wiser course of action and walked away from the area. Ryan tried to handle the situation and continued to insist that Zenrot should have a break before he's sent to the battlefield. As Ryan moved forward to get closer to Arashi, Zenrot placed his hand on Ryan's chest. They looked at each other and, without a word, Zenrot smiled weakly and nodded. Ryan could tell what he was trying to say. *Everything is fine, major.*

Zenrot turned his head and took a step forward. "All right, what are your orders, general?"

"*Tch.* That's better. Come, we must discuss some plans for our next attacks against Sentry Run." Arashi started heading to his office and Zenrot followed behind.

"Wait!" Ryan shouted to stop them. "There's one thing I must give him. Another weapon Grim and I made for Zenrot."

"I don't remember there being a *second* weapon."

"There wasn't," he said nervously. "But with all the strength Zenrot has… we decided to give him a sword. Sharp enough that it can slice anything. Even Sentry Run's robots."

Arashi looked at Zenrot, then at Ryan. He stared, expressionless, and no one could tell what he was thinking. "I hope this is not an excuse for you to mess around," Arashi spat, breaking the silence. He turned around and signaled his bodyguard to follow behind. "You have him until tomorrow night. After that, Zenrot comes with me and you go back to training recruits, do you understand?"

Ryan lowered his head. "Yes, sir."

"Good. I'll be in my office." Arashi left with his bodyguards.

When they were far away, Zenrot turned to Ryan and smirked. "*Tch.* For an old man, you have some balls, major."

"Well… That's what happens when I've spent months training you." They both started laughing. Ryan placed his hand over Zenrot's shoulder, and they started walking together. "Come, we're visiting Grim. I *do* have something for you. Plus, we have to get your gear before it gets dark."

***

Zenrot and Ryan arrived at the workshop. Grim was finishing the small details on the armor, but it was ready for Zenrot to wear. He had a gardbrace on his shoulders, a vambrace, and greave on his legs. The body armor was lightweight enough to cover his upper body without hindering his movement, though some places—the upper arms, space from his hips to his thighs, and his head—were exposed so he could move freely. Zenrot decided to wear black, fingerless gloves to feel comfortable holding any weapon.

"We're all set," Grim said. Sitting on a box and adjusting the leg pieces, Ryan was helping with the back part of the armor. He placed it on a table to adjust the sizing, and Zenrot noticed he was working some straps on the back to help Grim prepare Zenrot for battle.

"For a moment I thought you'd made an excuse to Arashi," Zenrot said.

"Since when do I make excuses?" Ryan said, scolding Zenrot. He felt ashamed for asking. "But," Ryan continued, "it was also so you could rest. But I was not lying about one thing." Ryan turned to face Grim. "Where did you put the sword?"

"It's on top of the cabinets." Grim stopped his work to look directly at Ryan. "Are you sure on giving your sword to the boy?"

"Yes... I think it is time I let it go. Besides, I'm sure it will be in good hands." Ryan went to the cabinet and struggled to reach the top for a moment, before he finally pulled something down. "Damn, it's heavy! I don't know how I can still lift this thing!"

The sword was covered in a sheet. Ryan walked slowly towards Zenrot and placed the sword on top of the table in front of him. "This," he said gently, "was something that's been passed down through my family for generations. It came from my grandfather to my father, from my father to me, and then to my… son." There was pain in his voice, but everything made sense to Zenrot now: why Ryan had been harder on Zenrot than anyone else. Why he was always brash and cold to people. Zenrot understood just by hearing the pain in Ryan's voice—the voice of a man who had lost his child.

He moved the sword closer to Zenrot. "This has been used only for good. Always fighting for the rights of my people and mutants. It has so much value to me and it's a shame that it's been put away for years." Ryan looked up to Zenrot, directly meeting his gaze. "I want you to have it and continue my legacy."

Zenrot shook nervously and took few steps away. "I—I can't!" he mumbled. "I can't accept this. It means a lot to you. Why give it to me?" he asked, worried and concerned.

"Because… I know you have good intentions," the major said peacefully.

"How can you be so sure?"

"Because you remind me of my son." Zenrot opened his eyes widely as Ryan looked back at his sword. "He was always positive. Never backed down, even during his hardest training he would always stand and fight. If he fell, he rose back up, no matter how difficult the situation was. He wanted to fight for the rights of mutants, which was ironic because he was human." He laughed softly. "But he knew it was the right thing to do. He was the one who motivated me to look out for everyone, not just regular humans." Ryan looked at Zenrot again. "And looking into your eyes, I see the same goal." He smirked, tapping with his fingers at the sheet covering the sword. "Plus, I can't use it anymore. I'm too old to lift this crap!"

Zenrot laughed a little and got closer to the sword. He removed the sheet and could immediately see the blade shine. It was a black and violet blade. The cross-guard of the sword was an inch long and eight inches thick. There was a symbol of a shield and a sword on the center of the rain guard. Zenrot lifted the sword by the grip and shifted it around to examine closely. The sword was five feet long. He tried to bend it and Ryan noticed his intention. "Don't worry, the sword will not be easy to break."

"That sword was made of the best carbon steel," Grim said while finishing with his gadgets. He walked to one of the worktable areas. Next to one of the workspaces was a scabbard for the sword with a long belt attached, so Zenrot could wear it and keep the sword safe. Grim grabbed it and walked to Zenrot, explaining, "The cross-guard is custom made to maintain the blade in its place." Grim handed the scabbard over while looking at the sword. With another look back at Ryan, he added, "his grandfather made a strong sword, indeed. That blade is so sharp that even looking at it can cut you easily."

"And heavy too," Zenrot added. He grabbed it with both hands, then switched it to his right hand, then tossed it to his left hand. "I mean, it's not heavy for me... but how come you and your family would pass this massive weapon on for generations? This thing looks hard to handle."

"With a lot of training and dedication over time," Ryan said proudly. "And, well... definitely not carrying it with one hand like you're doing right now."

Zenrot turned the sword around slowly to give it one last look. "I love it." He grabbed the scabbard and smoothly slid the sword inside before putting on the belt over his shoulder and resting the scabbard on his back.

"Promise me one thing," Ryan said. "No matter how difficult your journey may become... you will always stand for what is right."

"I promise. Thanks for everything, Ryan."

"Of course. Plus, my title as a major was on the line," he added sarcastically as he walked to the exit door. "Well, you're all set. We'd better get going. Tomorrow will be your last day of training."

"All right!" Zenrot sped towards Ryan but stopped halfway, turned to Grim, and bowed. "Thank you for all you've done for me."

"No problem, lad! Need any extra gadgets or weaponry, make sure to come around before—"

An alarm began sounding. Sirens all over Art Gun's base erupted in an announcement.

"ALL SOLDIERS OF ART GUN HEAD TO THE MAIN ENTRANCE! SENTRY RUN'S TROOPS ARE APPROACHING! REQUEST ALL SOLDIERS AT THE ENTRANCE IMMEDIATELY!"

They're invading again! Zenrot had a hunch about what type of enemy they were going to face: more robots. It could be Golems, Spartans, or maybe even something worse. Zenrot knew the soldiers couldn't hold the robots back on their own. He needed to help, and fast.

"I'm sorry but I must help the soldiers!"

"Zenrot, wait!" Ryan shouted as Zenrot put the holster on his waist and the scabbard on his back. "You just finished all of your training, maybe it's best to find the other mutants—"

"There isn't time!" Zenrot screamed. "If I don't help now, many people will die. I'm sorry, Major…" Zenrot turned around and busted through the door on his way to the battlefield. He sprinted as fast as he could to reach on time, passing civilians running away from danger on his way.

As he approached the main gate, he could see Golems and Spartans fighting the soldiers. Spartans were shielding against Art Gun's machine guns and explosions while the Golems swarmed the base, swinging their arms to hit any soldiers in the way. Two of Art Gun's helicopters were shooting the Golems from above and managed to take three of them down while Zenrot watched. In response, a Golem joined its hands together to form a giant weapon, which quickly started charging with energy to shoot.

"ELIMINATING AIR SUPPORT IN THREE… TWO… ONE…" The Golem shot a blast energy directly at the first helicopter. It fell all the way down and into a building. The crash blew it into pieces; the rotor blades flew clear away from the wreckage, adding to the destruction. While the Golem was busy shooting the second helicopter, another turned its left arm into a machine gun and focused on shooting at the civilians. The robot was killing them one by one, systematically, as they tried to run away.

A War For Mutants - The New Soldier

No! Everyone is in trouble!

Zenrot stopped at a distance, took out his revolver, and aimed at the Golem shooting the civilians. "Let's put this beauty to good use." He charged the revolver with his energy, feeling the cylinder of the gun almost expanding to its limits. Zenrot slowly squeezed the trigger, releasing the shot and putting a bullet through the Golem's chest before it could attack more soldiers. The blast left a giant hole in the robot, and the Golem slowly fell to the ground. "Holy shit!" Zenrot said, enlightened.

After the Golem was taken down, all the other robots turned their heads to face Zenrot.

"ALERT... MUTANT DETECTED... THREAT MASSIVE..." one of the robots shouted. All the Golems simultaneously raised their left arms, which were reconfiguring into machine guns.

"Oh, shit..." Zenrot dashed to the side as the Golems started firing. A hail of bullets followed Zenrot as he ran. Quickly gazing back, he saw some bullets hitting the ground as they followed him. The robots were correcting their aim and getting closer to him. Glancing around, he saw a two-story building made of cement and adjusted his run toward it. He managed to get around a corner and hide behind before any bullets caught up with him. A few seconds later, the Golems stopped shooting.

Zenrot leaned around the corner to take a quick look, but the Golems started shooting again and a swarm of projectiles tore into the side of the building near the corner he was peering out from. He ducked back into cover, coming up with another plan.

Zenrot threw a punch against the wall and made a hole at the back side of the building. He ducked in and found a stairwell to the second floor while the Golems were distracted. He charged the revolver as he ran upstairs, looking around in frantic agitation. After a moment, Zenrot spotted a window. Looking out through it, he had an overhead angle on the Golems. He took aim at the Golems, then released the charged shot.

"Eat this, metalheads!" Zenrot followed the first blast with several other shots at the Golems, putting another one out of commission. The Spartans gathered and stood on the mechanized forces front line, protecting the Golems with their shields. Zenrot's energy bullet managed to break some of the shields, but the damage was dramatically reduced for having to punch through them. He wasn't inflicting any critical harm whatsoever on the robots anymore. "Great…"

Zenrot made a quick look around the battlefield. The soldiers had fallen back and taken cover, but the Golems were still shooting at them. One soldier after another was falling, wounded or dead…

"We need backup!" a soldier shouted. "Where are the rest of the mutants?"

"Outside the base!" another soldier shouted back. "They're on their way to help, but at this rate they're going to show up to save a pile of dead bodies! We'll be executed if we don't think of some—*Ugh!*" Many bullets tore through the body before he could finish his sentence.

That wasn't a good sign. Zenrot raised his revolver once again and charged the gun with energy until the cylinder felt full. He took the shot, a huge blast of energy careening toward the Spartans. The energy blew four or five Spartans—Zenrot couldn't tell for sure with everything going on—away with only one bullet. He quickly took cover and took a moment to breathe. He felt exhausted. He now understood what Ryan had meant about being careful about using his abilities. It could drain him physically until he passed out, or worse, to death.

Zenrot was breathing desperately and took a few moments to inhale and exhale gently.

"ELEMINATING MUTANT IN THREE... TWO..."

"Shit!" Zenrot threw himself to his feet and sprinted out of the building. As he jumped outside, a massive amount of energy burst through the building. One Golem took the shot, while three Spartans were approaching to attack. Zenrot stood his ground, holding the handle of his sword with his right hand and waiting for the Spartans to come closer. The leading Spartan, ahead of the two others that were following, held the spear high and then threw it from above.

Zenrot waited a few seconds, then dashed toward the spear and dodged it. He snatched the spear with his left hand, then turned around to stab the Spartan with it. He used the momentum to draw the sword of his scabbard and spin into a horizontal blow, slicing the Spartan in half with one swing. He put the sword back into his scabbard, grabbed the shaft of the spear in the air and, with half the Spartan still attached, threw it at the others. Zenrot drew his revolver and shot at the broken Spartan's power core, triggering a huge explosion that consumed the other two Spartans. Smoke spread all over the center of the battle, but as it started fading away the Golems were aiming at Zenrot's position. He was exposed to all of the attacking robots.

"INITIATE SHOOT—"

The Golems were stopped by bursts of gunfire coming from the other soldiers of Art Gun from their various hiding spots, giving Zenrot some time to make a run for it. The robots turned around and started shooting back at the soldiers with their machine-gun hands, and a few of the soldiers were taken out. Zenrot sprinted his way to the Golems as Spartans landed in front of him, swinging with the shields to attack. He quickly crossed his arms in front of his body to block but was pushed heavily back by the blow. The Spartans raised their spears and shot energy blasts from the blades. Zenrot was barely fast enough to draw his sword in time to block all the energy blasts.

His arms were shaking, and his legs trembled with every step. *There are so many robots inside Art Gun's base!* One Golem switched its arm to a canon, charging enough energy to blow Zenrot away with a single blast. He raised his gun to aim back but couldn't keep his hand steady. He was struggling to guide his energy to charge his weapon. The soldiers couldn't stand against the robots, and the other mutants hadn't arrived on time. It occurred to Zenrot that this was going to be their last stand. He looked away and closed his eyes, unable to fight back and accepting his defeat.

The robot finished charging the canon… *BOOM!*

Zenrot was still standing. He gently opened his eyes as he raised his head to look. Fire was spreading through the area, and a few robots had been destroyed. Trucks came screeching into the battlefield and parked close to Zenrot. Soldiers swarmed out of them with machine guns, focusing their fire on just a few of the robots at a time to break the line and push them back. When Zenrot took a closer look, Ryan was on top of one of the trucks with a smoking rocket launcher in hand.

"If you think I was going to let you die here you're mistaken!" Ryan shouted as he reloaded the rocket launcher. "These robots are programmed to kill as much as they can until they're out of ammo—energy or regular ballistics!" Ryan rapidly sighted down the barrel and loosed another shot from the rocket launcher.

A group of Spartans gathered together to block the rocket with their shields. They were pushed back but resisted the damage from the explosion itself. Ryan snapped his attention to Zenrot. "We'll give you cover against the Golems when they show themselves! You take care of the Spartans!"

Zenrot nodded, confirming, and rushed to the robots.

"All soldiers focus on the Golems! Fire at any Spartan that decides to shoot Zenrot with their spears! Understood?" Ryan screamed.

"Yes, sir!" all the soldiers shouted in return.

Zenrot ran directly to the Spartans, bringing his right arm up to hold the handle of the sword, ready to draw it. The Spartans moved aside, still holding their shields for cover, giving the Golems space to shoot at Zenrot. Ryan took the opportunity and shot with his rocket launcher, hitting a Golem right in the head.

"Open fire!" Ryan shouted ferociously. The soldiers unleashed with their rifles and machine guns, forcing the Spartans to come together with other robots to shield them from the storm of incoming bullets. Zenrot was finally able to close the distance and, putting the revolver on his holster, unsheathed his sword. With two hands, he made a single swing against the robots with all his strength. The heavy weapon sliced against, into, and then through the shields. The momentum from his swing continued to propel the blade, and the heavy weapon tore through the metal parts of the Spartans standing in front. He slashed again as he moved, twisting and transferring the blade to just his right hand. As the sword continued its destructive arc through the robots, Zenrot struck a Spartan in the upper part of its torso with his left fist, blowing it, and the two Golems beside it, away.

"Zenrot, duck!" Ryan screamed. Zenrot immediately crouched. A spear passed through the space he had just been, almost having stabbed through the back of his head. He grabbed the spear while turning himself to face the Spartan, stabbing forward with his sword. The weapon connected and crushed vital machinery inside the Spartan, shutting it down completely.

The Golems rapidly adjusted their aim for Zenrot. Taking cover from the barrage, he used the Spartan's body as a shield. The soldiers kept shooting, but the cover fire was no longer having much of an effect. Zenrot held his ground.

One Golem stopped shooting and fell flat to the ground, then another one. Zenrot heard strong gunshots and took a quick look around. Glancing across the soldiers and their positions, he saw Ryan with a heavy sniper rifle.

"*Heh.* Thanks, Major! I owe you one!" Zenrot shouted with excitement.

"Word of advice… That's how you properly hit someone in

the head!"

"Really? You're giving me a lecture no— *agh!*"

"Zenrot!"

Zenrot was knocked sprawling by a Spartan's shield, rolling away across the ground. The Spartan rushed after him at full speed with its spear to stab Zenrot. He rolled himself to face the sky, but his eyes were looking at the Spartan. He snatched the revolver from his hip and started firing from close range with his energy. The metal was sinking inward, but the shots did not do enough damage to penetrate deep into the core. As the Spartan grew ever closer to deliver the killing blow onto Zenrot, it was abruptly pushed to one side. A truck screeched to a halt in front of Zenrot—and between him and the robot.

Ryan leapt from the driver's seat, dragging another rocket launcher from the passenger seat behind him. "Go to hell!" He shot the Spartan, but the robot was close enough for him and Zenrot to feel the pressure from the explosion. He quickly offered his hand to help Zenrot stand up.

"Are you all right?"

"Been better." Zenrot grabbed Ryan's hand, and both slid into cover behind the truck. They could feel the impact of bullets hitting the other side of the truck.

"This is Astred Mackol, can anyone copy? Over?" Someone spoke through Ryan's radio inside the truck. *"Me and the other mutants are fighting outside Art Gun's base. Can someone tell me what's the status inside? Over."*

Ryan threw himself into the truck and grabbed the communicator's handset. "This is Major Ryan Venango. We're holding our ground against the Golems and Spartans, but reinforcement just keep coming!"

"Roger that! We're eliminating most we can outside, but it'll be difficult for us to help inside the base! There's a lot of robots for us to handle!" Ryan could hear the gunshots over the radio circuit. It seemed like the other mutants wouldn't be able to help. Everything seemed lost for Ryan: fire and gunshots were spreading all over the area and reinforcements kept being wiped out before they could make an impact. Zenrot took a quick look at the Major, realizing that he seemed spaced out and traumatized.

He took out his revolver and charged with all the energy he could, until he felt the pistol at its limit. Zenrot stood as he aimed at the robots' position. He released the massive energy burst and hit a robot in the center of their formation. An explosion occurred, scrapping what looked to be a cluster of ten more robots in the process. Taking advantage of the diversion, he rushed into the truck and took the communicator out of Ryan's hand.

"This is Zenrot Bellator, member of the MSF," he said through the radio, "I'm holding my ground the best I can. Have you called for air support to assist outside the base?"

"We did!" Astred shouted while the noise of metal stressing, then breaking came in behind him. *"But Arashi is holding them for the moment! We need to wipe out as many Golems as we can, otherwise they will shoot down the helicopters!"*

"What if—*agh!*" Bullets tore into the side of the truck. Zenrot charged a small portion of energy in his revolver and returned fire rapidly with many smaller energy bullets to stun the robots. "What if I send the soldiers I've got in the battlefield to help you guys out?"

"Any help will suffice! But what about you—"

"Don't you worry about it!" Zenrot gazed at Ryan and a small smirk grew across his face. "The major and I got this." Ryan was surprised at how confident Zenrot was. So much had changed over these past months. Even if it seemed like they were running out of options, he wasn't going to give up without a fight. "Think you can keep the robots away once reinforcements arrive?"

"Yes!" An explosion occurred in the background. *"One of us will spread an intense field of fire all around Art Gun to prevent any robots invading the base once all the soldiers arrive. If they pass through it, they'll melt completely."*

"Understood. I'll clear the path for the soldiers so they can reach your location and wipe the remaining robots inside base. Wait for my order to lay the fire."

"Roger that! Wish you the best of luck on your own, Zenrot! Out!" Astred left the radio call.

"Here's the plan," Zenrot said to Ryan as he kept shooting with his revolver at the robots. "I'll destroy the robots as I'm on the run. You give me some cover fire while I sprint towards them."

"Are you insane?" Ryan screamed. "You'll be completely exposed to the enemy!"

"I can run fast enough to dodge most of their shots! I just need them distracted so I can destroy them up close!"

"But—"

"There's no time!" Zenrot shouted as he looked the major straight in the eyes. "I need you to trust me on this one. Can you do that, sir?"

Ryan came back to his senses and nodded. "Everyone listen up!" he screamed to all the remaining soldiers nearby. "All soldiers reconvene outside the base and prevent any more robots from getting inside! Grab any functional vehicle and head out now! Zenrot and I will take care of the remaining robots… Understood?"

"Yes, sir!"

Ryan pointed at one soldier. "You! Get over here!" The soldier sprinted, staying low to avoid getting hit. "You will drive my truck while I give Zenrot some cover fire!" Ryan jumped into the passenger seat while the soldier crawled into the driver's seat. He started the truck and started driving along the eastern perimeter of the base while Zenrot sped along the western border. He ran ahead to the remaining Spartans, and Ryan sprayed suppressing fire with an automatic rifle to make the Spartans unable to maneuver freely. They were stuck between covering themselves with their shields or taking the deluge of lead the major was unleashing.

Zenrot took the opportunity to engage. He reached the Spartans and swung with his sword, cutting down two robots and their shields. Another Spartan threw a spear at Zenrot, but he crouched fast enough to dodge. The mutant turned around while drawing his revolver and blasted the Spartan with an energy shot. Zenrot slid the sword into his scabbard, grabbed one of the severed robots with one hand, and ran forward.

The Golems were shooting at Zenrot, but he used the malfunctioning robot as a shield. While Zenrot approached, Ryan was on the other side with the truck still moving.

"Stop the car!" Ryan screamed, prompting the driver to stomp on the brake. He climbed out of the truck with the rocket launcher, once again reloaded, in his hands. "Oh no you won't!" He fired the weapon, and the explosive projectile blew up a couple more of the robots. Zenrot threw the partial Spartan he had been carrying at more of the Sentry Run forces and shot the energy core, making the explosion even bigger.

All the vehicles following Zenrot stopped, waiting for the smoke to vanish before they went ahead. Zenrot opened his eyes widely once the haze cleared. Hundreds of Golems and Spartans were continuing to advance towards the army. *There are so many.*

"This is Astred!" The voice crackled through Ryan's radio. *"We either need the reinforcements to stop these robots from approaching the base… or I give the order to start the heat, but you'll have to deal with the robots that make it inside while MSF spreads the fire!"*

Zenrot wanted to send the reinforcements for the mutants and soldiers fighting outside the base, but it seemed impossible. He wouldn't want soldiers to waste their ammunition because they would need it for the enemies outside. Zenrot took a quick look at the soldiers. Everyone was shooting at the robots and using rocket launchers and explosives where they could, since that was most effective against them. Even Ryan was putting the rocket launcher he'd requisitioned—or more likely just snatched, Zenrot knew—through its paces. Art Gun was blowing up robot after robot, but the shield wall made by the Spartans was guarding them and the Golems behind them well. Everyone inside the base may be able to hold things with Zenrot's help, but he found himself increasingly concerned for the people fighting outside. He was desperate for a solution to save everyone.

"I need an update now!" Astred shouted through the communicator.

"This is Ryan speaking... light it up—"

"Wait!" Zenrot shouted, finally having an idea. "I'll make a path for everyone to pass."

"HOW?" Ryan screamed. "The robots keep coming through the main entrance! We've done everything we could!"

"Not everything..." Zenrot took out his revolver. His red eyes shone brighter, and intense purple energy began to flow from his hand as he charged the gun. The cylinder kept expanding, growing more and more until it reached its limits. He aimed at the center mass of the advancing robot line. "Let's see if this baby can hold as much as Grim mentioned..."

"Zenrot, don't! If you use that much energy it could kill you!"

"If I don't do this now... we could die either way, and so would those fighting outside. Better just me than all of us." Zenrot looked at the Major and gave him the brightest smile he could. "Thank you for training me for the better." Zenrot focused back on the robots. The gun felt like it was about to break from all the energy it was consuming. "For a better life... and a better world!"

Zenrot squeezed the trigger. An intense, sustained energy blast came from the revolver, burning through the space between armies on its way to hit the Spartans. The mechanized invaders covered the line with their shields to weather the energy. The wave grew closer and closer...

BOOM!

The energy seemed to vaporize the shields and, not even seeming to dissipate, every single robot who had been behind them. The bullet didn't stop, either. Zenrot's shot devastated the Sentry Run forces until it reached the main entrance of the gate. Robots exploded in its wake.

"Everyone started moving outside! Go, go, go!" Ryan screamed. The soldiers turned on their vehicles and followed their way to the main gate, without getting close to the energy wave Zenrot had unleashed. It was still burning through the battlefield from the end of his weapon.

"What the hell is that?!" Astred shouted through radio.

"That's the signal! Tell your friend to prepare the flames!"

"Roger!"

"Come on Zenrot, just hold a little longer..."

Zenrot, holding the gun with one hand, had to raise the other to keep the gun steady. After a few seconds, the energy started to fade. His hands started to shake, but he had a smirk on his face. The last few robots left in the field were being finished off by the soldiers on their way by as the trucks sped outside the base. As Zenrot watched the trucks getting further away, his vision started getting blurry. His body felt numb.

"ZENROT!" He could hear Ryan's voice like an echo. Taking a few steps ahead, he fell onto his knees and landed hard on the ground. His eyes fluttered shut, and everything went dark.

CHAPTER ELEVEN

Zenrot slowly woke up. He was lying on a bed with patches all over his upper body and bandages on his hands. Looking at his surroundings, Zenrot recognized the insides of a medical tent. More patients were being attended to because of the fight. With full consciousness, he sat up, agitated when the doctors stopped him from getting out of bed.

"Sir, you need to rest," one of the field doctors said, "you unleashed quite an intense amount of energy and drained yourself completely, almost fatally."

"Screw that…" He moved to the side, trying to bypass the medic who wasn't letting him leave. "I need to help the rest of the men out there. I need to—"

"You need to do nothing," Ryan said as he walked inside the tent, "because the fight is over."

"Major Ryan! What happened? How long have I been out?"

"About an hour. The Golems and the Spartans have been taken care of."

"I see…" Zenrot exhaled softly, relieved that the fight was over. "But… how did we win, exactly?"

"Well, after your heroic effort, the rank-and-file soldiers managed to reach the exterior of the base. They helped the other mutants, one of whom used all his energy to release a huge fire around Art Gun. He transformed it into something like a shield. Those robots that tried to walk through it got melted, and that gave enough time for air support to come in and take care of the rest."

"Damn. That other mutant must have used quite a lot of energy, too." Zenrot sounded impressed. "Who was that?"

"His name is Frederick Crossvelt," Ryan clarified.

"I see, wish I could thank him for his effort."

"He was in one of these tents, but he just left. However, he's a member of the MSF, so you'll probably meet him later." Zenrot put his hand on his stomach, feeling an intense growling. Even over the noise of caring for injured soldiers, Ryan could faintly hear it. He gave Zenrot an expressionless stare. "After all that fight and energy expenditure… I thought you would be exhausted, not hungry."

Zenrot rubbed the back of his head nervously. "*Heh.* Anyone got any food around here by any chance?"

The medics and doctors shook their heads, confirming that none had any food. Ryan rubbed his fingers on his eyes, amazed at Zenrot's behavior. "You know… you had me worried back there." He removed his fingers and looked straight at Zenrot. "You ran away to fight the robots, many which were difficult to defeat alone. Yet you risked your life even though all seemed lost…"

"But, sir—"

"Let me finish!" Ryan snapped. Zenrot lowered his head. "Not only that, but you also used so much energy that it drained you completely. The doctors told me your heartrate was low and could probably end up in a coma. I was afraid you might never wake up; that you ended up dead. You… you are unbelievable, you know that?"

"Sorry, Major…"

"Even after disobeying my orders and making reckless decisions, I must say… that I'm very proud of you."

Zenrot looked up, gasping in surprise. For the first time ever, he heard very clearly what Major Ryan said. After all this time, he had never been more relieved to hear those words from his teacher. He felt proud at his choices. "You really mean that?" Zenrot asked to be certain.

"I do. Thanks to you a lot of people are safe. For now, at least."

"*Heh.* Thanks, Major." Zenrot gently stood up, reaching for his sword and gun. "So… does this mean I can get a reward?" After he grabbed his weapons, he turned, waving his hands with excitement. "Oh, oh! Maybe we can get some food at Han's place. I could use some of that in my stomach after a tough fight."

"You really think, after all this mess, he will be working in his restaurant?"

"I mean… Mr. Han is a very committed man when it comes to food."

After a moment, Ryan conceded. "You have a point…" He

walked outside the tent, checking to make sure no one was nearby. As he walked out, Ryan signaled Zenrot with his hands to follow. *Why is the major being so sneaky?* They passed rows of tents, avoiding all the soldiers and doctors, and made sure that neither of them were spotted. Ryan looked ahead and saw a truck along with two soldiers speaking to one another. "Wait here."

Ryan went ahead alone, approaching the soldiers. Zenrot couldn't hear their conversation from where he waited. It took a while, but one soldier handed Ryan the keys to the truck and they both went their way. He opened the passenger door and quickly signaled Zenrot, who ran as quietly as he could and got inside. Ryan sat in the driver's seat and started the truck.

"Mind me asking what that was all about?"

"Arashi ordered supervision kept on you."

"Meaning...?"

"He wanted to make sure that, after you woke up, no one was allowed to come close to you. You are now considered of great value to the company after that fight. Arashi wanted you directly at his office."

"*Heh.* And you decide to break that rule?"

"At this moment, I had to. I know we're at war, but I believe you need to recover properly. You already burned enough energy. I don't need Arashi to overdo his demands on you."

"Spoken like a true major."

Ryan took a deep breath, trying to relax himself from the decision he just made. "Hope Han has some left over for us."

***

Zenrot and Ryan managed to get some food from Mr. Han. Surprisingly, he was still at work, as if he wasn't afraid enough to leave his restaurant. Zenrot and Ryan weren't eating inside, however; they ate in the back of the truck, parked behind the restaurant. Ryan was still on the lookout so that no one spotted them while they ate. This was a totally new life experience. Zenrot had never expected the major to break his moral code.

Both were eating beef and fries. Mr. Han came from the back door of the restaurant, holding a trash bag with one hand and a gallon of water in the other. He threw the trash bag away while on his way to deliver the gallon. He saw Zenrot quickly devouring his food while Ryan was eating modestly, by comparison.

"Well, glad you boys are eating good." Mr. Han handed over the water.

"Thanks, Mr. Han! Food is good as always."

"Well, good thing I've always been committed to my job when it comes to cooking."

"I still think that you should've evacuated," Ryan said as he cleaned his mouth with a napkin. "Many people died during the invasion of the robots."

"It is a tragedy indeed, but I couldn't leave my restaurant. I have done so much in here, served a lot of people." Mr. Han gazed at Ryan. "So how will you handle Arashi once he finds out you took Zenrot away? You know how difficult he gets when someone disobeys his orders."

"*Mphm*. Don't remind me... Arashi already wanted me to deliver Zenrot before the invasion started. When he finds out about this, he'll be a pain in the ass."

Zenrot chuckled. "It isn't something you haven't handled before. Right, Major?"

"That is correct." Ryan finished his plate and looked at his watch. It was almost midnight. "We better get moving." Ryan stood up with his plate in hand. "You have a big day tomorrow, Zenrot." Ryan hopped from the back of the truck, asked Zenrot for his plate, and moved to enter the kitchen through the back door. Before he could get there, he was stopped by Mr. Han.

"Oh no you don't!" Han took the plates out of Ryan's hands. "You go and take Zenrot to his quarters! I'll take care of the plates."

"At least let us help you a bit with the store for staying so late to feed us."

"We?" Zenrot hesitated. "But I'm tired—" Ryan glared at Zenrot fiercely. That they were even eating at Han's place was because Zenrot was the hungry one. "Su—sure."

"Nah, don't worry about me," Mr. Han said lightly, "I'm already finishing what's left to inside. A couple plates isn't going to take too much time." Mr. Han waved a hand as a sign for Ryan to leave. "Go! Don't make your situation more complicated than it already is."

Ryan nodded in gratitude and went to the driver's side of the truck. Zenrot waved his goodbyes and locked the back, then jumped to the passenger's seat. "Careful, Zenrot! You nearly hit me with the sword."

"Sorry, Major." Zenrot laughed weakly. Ryan started the car and navigated the vehicle to the mutant's residence. On their way, Zenrot watched through the window at how people were cleaning up the debris. A few locals were repairing the tents that were damaged and picking up pieces of different robots. It felt like it was a new rebuild of Art Gun.

Zenrot thought it was lucky that the fight had been won today, but the war was far from over. Sentry Run had reached more than once into their base. This time, many lives were at stake. Many of them died in battle, but some died with no intention of fighting—they had just been trying to find a place to live until peace was finally secured. So far, it seemed impossible for anyone to live peacefully. As long as Sentry Run stood, no one was safe.

"We're here," Ryan finally said after a few minutes of driving. Zenrot got out of his thoughts and looked through Ryan's window, seeing his building. He climbed out of the truck and walked to Ryan's side.

"Are you sure you'll be all right with Arashi?"

"Well, it isn't something I haven't handled before."

"Fair enough…" Zenrot said lightly, still preoccupied with Ryan's wellbeing.

"Don't worry, I'll be all right. You get the rest you need. Tomorrow will be a new path for you. There won't be any more training. You will be out in the field, dealing with dangerous enemies."

"Understood." Zenrot tapped his finger twice against the driver's door and walked away. Almost at the entrance of his quarters, he stopped. Zenrot turned half to one side to look at Ryan and gave a soft smile. "Hey, Major!" he shouted. "When this war is over, perhaps we should hang out sometime. You know… without the shooting and all that crap."

Ryan chuckled, finding it funny how Zenrot expressed himself. "Sounds like a plan. See you then." Zenrot nodded and stepped inside his residence.

Ryan was about to start the truck when he felt a presence in the dark. He looked up as someone slowly approached. When Ryan had a clear visual, he noticed it was one of Arashi's bodyguards. From his perspective it seemed they had just been passing by, but the bodyguard stopped in front of the truck.

"Good evening!" Ryan said. There was not a single word from the bodyguard. He heard footsteps from the side and one bodyguard stood outside his window. Ryan looked at the driver's side view mirror and saw two more approaching at the back. He looked to the bodyguard outside the window. "Is there a problem?" Ryan asked.

"General Arashi would like to speak with you at his office," the bodyguard said bluntly.

"All right…" Ryan answered in a muddled tone. "But does he need this many men to send me a message?"

"It's for precaution, sir. If you're so kind to get in the passenger seat, I'll take it from here." Ryan did as he was asked. One bodyguard got in the driver's seat and the other three climbed into the back of the truck. Ryan knew this was coming, and that Arashi would ask for his presence, yet it seemed so odd at how they had approached. He had no choice, Ryan couldn't disobey even if it was being delivered through a messenger. When Arashi said a single word, everyone followed orders.

After driving to the main building, Ryan stepped out of the

truck. One bodyguard took the lead as the others stood behind Ryan, making sure he walked ahead. Entering the headquarters building, there was no one working inside. It looked strange not seeing a single person working desperately at ending the war. Ryan couldn't remember a day when it was this empty.

Everyone arrived at the elevator and reached the last floor. When they arrived, Ryan and the bodyguards moved into the room. Arashi was sitting on his desk, tapping with his fingers on its surface. His face was calm, but also frightened. Something was off about him.

Ryan took a few steps forward. "Everything all right, General Arashi?" he asked.

"Ah yes…" He stood up and walked slowly towards Ryan. "How is our boy doing?"

"Zenrot? He's fine, probably in his bedroom sleeping."

"I see." They were face to face. "You gave him your precious toy, didn't you?" Ryan felt more anxious than ever.

"Ye—Yes, sir." He replied between his words. "It was a good thing I gave him the sword when I had the chance. He used it to his advantage in breaking the robots' defenses."

"*Mmm*. Perhaps you're right," Arashi spoke calmly, but tension crept into his voice, "or perhaps it was because you couldn't let him go? There were direct orders to deliver the boy to me after he woke, and yet… you took him on a trip for a meal. Am I right?"

Ryan was silent, speechless. Arashi knew everything about escaping the tents all along.

"There was no doubt that the sword is a good tool for Zenrot after his performance today. But I don't believe that the sword was given to him for his needs in battle in the first place."

"I don't follow, sir."

"I remember many years back... when your son was a soldier." Arashi walked back to his desk. "He preferred close combat instead of using a gun. He took special drugs provided by Mojo... drugs that gave him unique abilities over time. Pretending to be a mutant to symbolize our reason for fighting." He turned his eyes to Ryan. "But that's what got him killed, yes? Playing at being a hero."

The remark triggered Ryan and he took a step forward, agitated. "Don't you dare to talk—"

Arashi's bodyguards aimed at him with their heavy rifles, forcing him to a halt. One wrong move and he knew they'd blast him. "Or what, Major Ryan?" Arashi sat back at his desk with confidence. "Zenrot does remind you of your son, doesn't he? I can see why you're so attached to him. I know you have good intentions... but, like I said before, we're at war. I need my men sharp. That includes the mutants."

"I understand, sir... but I don't understand why you brought me here to disrespectfully speak about my son." He spoke nervously, yet with firm voice to maintain his posture and respect. "Besides, after tomorrow, Zenrot will be working with the MSF, so I won't be working with him anymore."

"That might be true... but you two are getting too attached. I need him focused. I need a strong mutant that can fight any threat in his path. A real soldier. A killing machine. I can't have him deeply emotional, Major. For the sake of this war, I need to take precautions." He snapped his fingers and some of his men forcefully grabbed Ryan. He tried to break free, but there were too many other men holding him tight.

"What are you doing?" he shouted fearfully. "I've been working for this army, fighting by your side my entire life. You think I would do something reckless to ruin it?"

"I've always trusted your loyalty, Major... But I must do what is right for this war and that boy is enough for me to win this."

"You don't care about his wellbeing, nor any other mutant's! You only care about winning this damn war! You will risk anyone's life just so you can say we saved the mutants when you're making them fight until they die. Aren't we supposed to fight to save *them* and prove humans and mutants can get along? They sound more like a tool for you."

"Whatever it takes to survive, Major." He lifted his hand, indicating to take Ryan away. The major tried to break free, but four soldiers took him away through the elevator. Arashi stepped quietly to his window to watch the base. He glanced at one of his bodyguards and motioned him near. Arashi ordered him to pick Zenrot up early tomorrow, and to bring him to his office with the other members of the MSF. The guard left and Arashi stood alone, watching the base from high above everyone else. "Tomorrow is the day Art Gun will finally have the best squad that has ever existed in history."

ACKNOWLEDGMENTS

Writing this book turned out to be quite a journey. Lot of challenges along the way, especially during the pandemic times. Those one-hour lunch break, writing every day and finding time to actually sit and write, even if it was just a few words, I couldn't let this story pass away. I am so grateful for the support I received along the way.

To my wife Yeshmarie, who sketches most characters to have a visual input of how they are presented. Which they totally worked! Always carry them close to me when it comes to working with the story and inspire me to write non-stop. Often when I was close to giving up on my story because I thought it wasn't going nowhere, she encouraged me to finish over and over until it was finally done, and for that, I am truly grateful.

To brother-in-law Bryan, who's been very supportive and always told me great suggestions for the story to be greater. Also, for listening to the story and reading it over and over until it sounded better.

To Steven, Jose, and Jan, who have been my beta readers, who been tortured with the first and second draft (sorry!) and pointed out where could the story stand out more and the errors along the way. They also been cheerleading and asking constantly for more content every single week. Chill guys, I'm flattered but one thing at a time haha.

Of course, my family and friends who supported me in the years I've been working with this book and further projects coming ahead. Which some insisted to publish my stories over and over, writing this book was a wonderful experience, but I was scared to publish since I was afraid it might not be enjoyable story, but I was so wrong when my beta readers and those who heard the story said otherwise, and for that I'm grateful.

To my editor Joseph Furmanick, who polish this story and made amazing suggestions to make the story ten times better. The developmental edit and line edit was outstanding, pointed out where things could take place as the story progressed. Thank you for the opportunity.

ABOUT THE AUTHOR

Alberto is a Puerto Rican author living in a small house on Trujillo Alto. He spent most of his time on Saturday morning in a library, either writing or drinking a cup of coffee while reading a good book. He has a degree in graphic design, loves video games, and if there's any free time available, he plays a bit of music. Alberto's favorite genres are sci-fi, fantasy, and thriller books.

Printed in the USA
CPSIA information can be obtained
at www.ICGtesting.com
LVHW050802060923
757303LV00007B/91